SEEKING CHARITY

JOSIE RIVIERA

INTRODUCTION

To keep up on newly released ebooks, paperbacks, Large Print Paperbacks, audiobooks, as well as exclusive sales, sign up for Josie's Newsletter today.

As a thank you, I'll send you a Free PDF ... The Beauty Of ...

Josie's Newsletter

Did you know that according to a Yale University study, people who read books live longer?

5 STAR READER REVIEWS

"This poignant love story is filled with adventure, intrigue and romance. Josie Riviera's writing evokes tender emotions and a deep understanding of God's love for us and our love for others. All of her books are a must-read for those who appreciate genuine love from a Christian perspective. Thank you Josie Riviera!"- Amazon Reviewer

"It was cool to read about the gypsy customs especially the broom for marriage. This was a clean second chance best friend's historical romance."- Amazon Reviewer

5.0 out of 5 stars
"An excellent book and beautiful storyline. I highly recommend that you get this book, I'm sure you will definitely enjoy it!"- Amazon Reviewer

This book is dedicated to all my wonderful readers who have supported me every inch of the way.
THANK YOU!

PRAISE AND AWARDS

USA TODAY bestselling author

#7 Amazon Bestseller British Literature Anthologies
#17 Amazon Bestseller Religious Short Stories

CHAPTER 1

 ales, 1812

"LET'S drink to a long and happy life for the bride and groom!"

Charity Weston stood at the edge of a smoky campfire with her Romany Gypsy tribe and raised her tankard of ale. Luca, the leader of their tribe, offered the toast in celebration for a *pliashka*, a betrothal agreement.

Miriah, the attractive bride-to-be, smiled radiantly at her intended groom, who grinned proudly at her. Both sets of future in-laws stood beside them. Miriah's dark brows and eyes dominated her features, accentuated by glossy ebony hair tied back with a vivid red headdress.

So unlike her own copper-colored hair, Charity thought, fingering her unmanageable ringlets.

As the tribesmen hooted and cheered, Charity joined in the chants of *sastimos*, good health, even as her cheeks flushed at the bawdy remarks laughingly called out to the couple.

In the glow of the firelight, she studied the Gypsy men and women assembled in a circle around the couple—the laugh lines etched in the corners of their mouths and the granite determination in their jaws, announcing their decision to live unrestrained from the constraints of 'civilized life'.

Several men with greying beards loudly shared opinions about where they should travel next and that they should leave within a fortnight. They'd stayed in one place long enough. In the meantime, Luca didn't respond as he bent to retrieve a bottle of brandy for the groom's father. The father then wrapped a handkerchief around the bottle as part of the pliashka.

These were the people Charity had grown to love. Their kindness, their traditions, their joy for life. They brought nothing with them when they traveled and simply adopted the traditions of wherever they made camp.

A clap of thunder reverberated, and the heavy wooden wagons, packed with garments and jewelries, creaked in response.

However, weather changes didn't deter the revelers. Besnik, one of the elders, took up a pipe whistle and began playing, whilst another grabbed his fiddle. Kezia, an elderly woman who was considered the *phuri dai*, someone who resolved conflicts with honor, clapped to the music and sang off-key. The melody was spirited yet emotional. Since the tribe had settled in Wales, their music had taken on a decidedly Welsh, Celtic quality.

Charity finished her ale. Intrigued, she watched as Miriah's future father-in-law secured a necklace around Miriah's throat. Made of a satin ribbon with gold coins, the necklace was a symbol of the matrimony bond.

"Remember." Kezia stepped forward and focused on Miriah, *"Ajsi bori lachi: xal bilondo, phenel londo."*

Charity grinned as she silently translated: "Such a daughter-in-law is good who eats unsalted food and says 'tis salted."

"Good advice!" A boisterous shout of approval came from the men and Charity gave her head a shake. Despite living with Gypsies for six years, the good-natured commotion and dust and brightly-colored gowns sometimes evoked a dreamlike blur of confusion.

And lately, it also brought a sense of detachment. The setting was so different from the proper English background of her childhood—high-waisted white muslin dresses, formals planned months in advance, country dances with their processional marches and ballet-style movements.

But that was all in the past.

Through a break in the surrounding woods, she peered toward a stone mansion, the Colchesters' grand country estate. The owners, James and Valentina, had invited the tribe to camp on their property. Mr. Colchester was wealthy landed gentry, and Valentina, a Gypsy woman. Despite society's rigid rules, they had fallen in love, married, and moved to Wales.

And it was marvelous here, Charity mused, scanning her surroundings. The rugged Welsh landscape alive with summer color, the sounds of the sea crashing to shore, the bright open sky shining at night with pinpoints of bright stars.

Why, then, could she think of little else than her former English home?

Lately, Wales induced a longing for her childhood she couldn't explain. She had spent many a summer in Norfolk by the sea when her mother was alive, she reasoned. Perhaps

3

'twas why these remembrances came with more and more frequency.

As the last of the tankards were emptied, she set down her own to refill an empty flask with more braggot, a honeyed Welsh ale. She handed the flask to Luca, who poured some into a tankard for himself, then offered the flask to the others. Grabbing a slab of bread, he glanced at her, a smile crossing his dark tanned features.

"Thank you, Charani."

As always, he called her by her Gypsy name.

With a nod, she turned, planning to assist the younger women roasting a hedgehog on a wooden spit.

"What is troubling you?" For such a commanding presence, he had the ability to move quietly and quickly. He'd come up behind her, and she hadn't noticed until he spoke. "This past fortnight, you are preoccupied."

She shrugged her bright-pink shawl tighter around her shoulders. The temperateness of summer promised another month of welcoming days, although the chill of a sea breeze hung in the air.

"'Tis nothing," she said.

He studied her face. "I watched you during the pliashka. Are you missing someone? Mayhap a man from a neighboring tribe? I saw you conversing with Petshah the last time we went to market."

"We met once and are only friends. Besides, isn't he at least thirty years my senior?"

And so heavy he could crush her. She didn't add that part.

"Age doesn't matter."

"Perhaps." She waited for Luca's response. She was twenty years old, and would soon be labeled a spinster if she didn't wed.

"He's made it known he's interested in you," Luca said.

She shook her head and didn't respond, knowing she was

4

no match for the bristle in Luca's deep tone, nor his persistence. She picked up a stick to turn the meat and began a casual conversation about the passing of summer and of Romany customs, particularly the pliashka.

Thankfully, the subject of spinsterhood wasn't mentioned, but her good luck didn't last. With a determined gleam in his dark eyes, Luca repeated his earlier question. "What troubles you, Charani?"

She turned her attention away from the hedgehog and faced Luca squarely. "Sometimes ..." Her voice dropped to a whisper. "I don't know where I belong anymore."

There. She'd blurted it, becoming more like a Gypsy every day. Gone were the days of well-bred protocol, the soft tone of an Englishwoman schooled to never share her opinions aloud. Conversely, within the tribe, she could speak her mind.

Luca nodded slowly, his gaze understanding. "I know the feeling."

The emotion in his admission struck her heart, making her ache all the more for things left behind long ago—a lavish home, a soft mattress, and sparkling clean bed linens.

Nay, she admonished herself. She was unappreciative for even thinking such thoughts. Luca's tribe had been benevolent, accepting her after the first Gypsy tribe she joined had moved to Scotland.

"How would someone like you, a Rom, know anything about not belonging?" she wanted to ask, although she said nothing. He was the head of the tribe for a reason. While brash, he took an interest in every tribesmen, listening intently, offering advice whenever asked. And although she'd heard rumors regarding his parentage, his past was never questioned.

He took several sips of ale and then lowered the heavy tankard. "Have you met Valentina?"

It was a strange change in subject, although Charity was grateful.

"Nay. Have you?"

"Aye. She was a childhood friend. Earlier this afternoon, I met her at the stables. She assured me we were welcome to remain as long as we wished."

"She's a proper lady now, married to landed gentry."

He shrugged. "She'll always be one of us, a Romany at heart."

Us. So Luca regarded Charity as a Gypsy. Noteworthy, because she looked nothing like them. Her skin was pale, her eyes a crystal-blue, the opposite of the tanned skin and piercing brown eyes of Luca and the others.

"Valentina is kind to allow us to camp on her husband's land," she said.

She waited for Luca's response. The smoky smells of wood campfires, cooking odors of fennel and garlic, hung in the air. Inside a crude stable, a spotted Welsh pony, small and sturdy, whinnied.

As always, Luca took his time, retying the green sash around his waist, running a hand along his buckskin breeches. It was his way, deliberating when he had something important to say. Years earlier, he had assumed the responsibilities of caring for the mostly elderly tribe without complaint, although he was only a young adult male himself.

"Would you like to meet her?" he finally asked.

"Valentina?" Charity scarcely noticed the encouragement in his tone, his voice nearly drowned out by several of the men near the campfire calling for more ale. "From the tales I've heard, she's a *drabardi*, a fortuneteller." She shook her head. "I don't want my fortune told. The Rom have taught me how to live in the present and trust myself and my instincts."

6

Although when she was younger, she had relied on God to carry her through the rough patches.

Nay. She corrected her thought. God had carried her through every patch, whether rough or smooth. When had she lost the faith she once held so strongly?

"Valentina is no longer a drabardi," Luca was saying. He sipped his ale, took a bite of bread, before continuing. "Valentina told me one of Mr. Colchester's acquaintances is looking for property in the area. She's invited them to stay for a fortnight."

"And?"

"And you can join them for a meal, or a game of whist, or whatever the English do to while away their time." He shrugged. "More important, 'twill give you an opportunity to converse with English men and women."

"I'm happy here with the Gypsies."

Firmly, he shook his head. "'Tis exactly what you need to bring pink color back to your cheeks. You've grown paler this season, despite the sun." Another sip, another bite. "Certainly an English lady like yourself grows weary of our Gypsy customs."

She frowned, reflecting on all he'd said. "I don't know Valentina."

"I'll introduce you."

"I haven't been invited."

"You will be."

"I won't fit in." She regarded her vivid orange gown. "I haven't conversed with any Englishmen besides shop owners in years."

"You'll like Valentina. She's adapted to the English ways and no longer believes in spirits."

"I don't believe in spirits, either."

"Mr. Colchester is a devout Christian and Valentina has

followed suit," Luca continued. "You are a Christian too, aye?"

Aye. Once. Long ago.

Since arriving in Wales, she heard the peal of church bells every Sunday. She had contemplated attending services, but always quelled the thought. She was a Gypsy woman now, and she'd enough of her tyrannical father's heavy hand, all in the name of God.

"Although I don't agree with Valentina's interest in Christianity," Luca added, "they are happy, and I am glad for them."

Charity couldn't be happy or sad for the Colchesters because she didn't know either of them, but she appeased Luca by agreeing.

A grin touched his lips. "So, you will consider my suggestion?"

Wrapping her arms around herself, she stared at the grand estate in the distance, the smoke billowing from enormous chimneys, the torchlights lit, the flickering light of beeswax candles through the windows.

"Of course," she replied. Inwardly, she'd already made up her mind. She couldn't attend a fancy dinner in such a grand house. Not wanting to spoil the pliashka with a disagreement, she decided to wait and tell Luca her decision come the morrow.

He surveyed her, apparently considering her reply. "Good. 'Tis settled." Abruptly, he swung around to rejoin the merriment by the campfire.

Immersed in her thoughts, she stared into the camp firelight, the festivities forgotten. Memories best hidden broke to the forefront. When she had run away from home, she had vowed to never look back.

She'd even changed her name to be doubly sure no one from England would ever find her.

* * *

A FEW HOURS LATER, long after she'd gone to her tent to sleep for the night, Charity awoke to a nightmare. Her eyes snapped open. Her heart beat heavily in her chest, her breathing quick. Something had brought her from a sound sleep to acute awareness.

She shot upright on her floor mattress. Judging from the angle of the moonlight spilling through her canvas tent, 'twas the middle of the night.

She flopped back, trying to get comfortable. With the sharp, chopped straw poking at her, comfort wasn't something that came easy. Still, she was safe, and in her familiar tent, the tent she had lived in for the past six years. Relieved, she swallowed. Her mouth was so dry.

She rolled onto her stomach and scanned the shadowy possessions she'd come to treasure. A small washbasin sat in a corner beside a water pitcher, a wooden stool placed nearby. A basket of blueberries she'd picked earlier in the day perched on a bench.

Her gown was draped on a table made of rough-hewn wooden planks.

She planned to wear it to market. Luca intended for the tribe to pick up supplies, which meant haggling for fresh vegetables and eggs whilst the boys and girls from the tribe stole jewelry from unsuspecting rich ladies to sell for coin.

Although Charity didn't condone stealing, she understood the necessity when supplies were low and jobs for Gypsies were nonexistent. Perhaps someday, the attitude toward Gypsies would change. The Colchester marriage was certainly an encouraging beginning to ending all the bigotry in the world.

Sweat gathered on her brow. Understandable, she rationalized, considering the close air in the tent. But it was more.

9

The nightmare had jarred her dreams, and more memories of her upbringing invaded her thoughts.

Why now? Wales had brought her great joy, yet the remnants of past fears sat on the edge of her consciousness. After all this time, she still felt her father's firm fingers pushing her down onto the cold stone floor of the linen closet. She still felt his hand strike her with such force, the air was knocked from her lungs.

When he punished her, which was often, her mind had gone over and over her mishaps.

Why was she being punished? Was she really that bad?

She did ride her horse for hours, but that wasn't a reason to be disciplined.

Daniel Hayward, a longtime friend from her village, oftentimes accompanied her on his horse. Those were carefree, happy times, she thought. Indeed, her father must have realized she and Daniel oftentimes lost track of time, laughing and racing each other through the woods and pastures that surrounded their respective homes.

She smiled, her heart swelling with the heartening remembrances. She and Daniel had talked endlessly of their childhood dreams and childhood pursuits.

Where was he now? she wondered. When she had left, he'd been eighteen, four years older than she. Despite that age difference, they got along wonderfully well together, although she sometimes overheard gossip in the village. Even Daniel's sister told Charity she made a fool of herself when she was with him, especially since she hunted him down to come riding with her.

That wasn't true. Daniel had always sought her, and he had clarified that fact on more than one occasion with his sister.

However, it *was* true that Charity couldn't help glancing at him whilst they rode. He was tall and good-looking, possessing the easy charm of the affluent, well-bred gentleman. She'd seen him grow from a lanky boy to a man, his shoulders broadening, his muscular legs clearly outlined in tightly-fitted leather breeches. And his eyes—a soft silver-grey, frequently sparking with mirth. He was handsome and self-assured, and she developed a crush for him. Although, of course, he never knew, for at the age of fourteen she was plain-featured, overly tall, and self-conscious.

She sighed. Hadn't they vowed to be best friends forever? She wondered if he remembered the day before she decided to run away. It had been her birthday, and she had chosen to spend part of the day with Daniel, riding horses and enjoying a picnic with friends and several chaperones.

After they returned to her home and before he left for his, Daniel leaned against an oak tree, so close to her she was afraid he could hear her pounding heart, and teased her that he'd beat her fair and square whilst they'd raced home.

"Please never forget me," she suddenly said.

"Why would I?" He raised his dark eyebrows. "You're not intending to leave me, are you?"

How had he known?

She hadn't answered, gazing up at the face she knew so well, hoping she could memorize it forever.

Lightly, he'd touched her cheek. "Where are you going?"

Away, she thought, briefly squeezing her eyes shut. *I don't want to leave you, but I must.*

On impulse, she stood on her toes and kissed him. In response, he'd stepped away and joked about how he would always beat her when they raced. She'd responded to his bantering with laughter.

At that point, her memories went from good to bad as she recalled her "transgressions," as her father labeled her wrongdoings. Oftentimes, he caught her dozing in church. When accused, she argued her good reasons because the vicar droned on for hours. Certainly her father would understand.

But he never did.

Instead, he forced her to kneel and recite Bible passages. Hadn't he known that by forcing her to recite a beloved verse, she would turn away rather than toward God? Hadn't he known she missed her mother as much as he did? She saw the telltale sorrow crossing his face whenever her mother's name was mentioned.

And her mother's name was also Charity. Many people commented on their resemblance. Charity had her mother's same unaffected beauty, hair color, and fiery, headstrong nature.

She pushed a strand of her unruly hair from her face. That was where the resemblance ended because, unlike her mother, Charity was an independent woman, relying on no one but herself.

Resolutely, she turned her thoughts from anything having to do with the English and her former life among them.

Closing her eyes, she courted sleep. A passage from Proverbs came, uplifting and encouraging.

"'Trust in the Lord with all thine heart; and lean not onto thine own understanding. In all thy ways acknowledge Him, and he shall direct thy paths.'"

She hadn't recited that particular Bible passage, or any Bible verse, in many years. Yet somehow, the prayer had drifted easily to her lips.

CHAPTER 2

*D*aniel Hayward assisted his sister, Penelope, into her carriage whilst she complained endlessly about the new cook she'd hired. A crisp morning breeze cooled the air, and the thistledown moving gently across the fields meshed with the scent of pine floating down the tall fir trees. In addition to their carriage, another coach carrying trunks, valises and Penelope's maid followed, along with two outriders, one riding in the front and the other bringing up the rear.

Daniel was staying for a month in Wales with Penelope and her husband, Theodore Huckabee. They'd been married for many years and were childless, a fact that bothered neither of them. For the most part, they lived completely separate lives.

Briefly, Daniel wondered how his parents would have felt about his sister's marriage. Years earlier, he'd overheard their quiet prayers that Penelope and Theodore would find true love. When they were alive, they often expressed their desire for grandchildren.

Their prayers hadn't been answered—neither by Penelope and Theodore, nor by him. At four and twenty years old, he had no desire to marry and sire children anytime soon.

"So, Daniel, what do you think of the property Theodore and I are looking at?" Penelope settled into the carriage and gathered her teal-blue satin gown about her. "Shall we purchase the estate or not?"

Theodore and Penelope had sought Daniel's advice concerning an investment property in Wales. The place had a shabby quality, having fallen into disrepair, and Theodore intended to purchase the home at a low bid, pay for some repairs, and then resell at a profit. In the meantime, Theodore and Penelope were renting a summer home nearby.

"The home needs work," Daniel began, smiling at his understatement. He took a seat across from her in the carriage, and the driver guided the pair of greys out of the Huckabees' drive.

"That's your assessment?" A look of sorely strained patience crossed his sister's pretty face. She shook back her long blonde curls, sending them trailing over her shoulders. A pearl comb kept the tresses back from her face.

"Your husband has a greater say. 'Tis merely my opinion."

"'Tis your professional opinion. Considering the wealth you've accumulated, Theodore values your insight." She sighed. "Although I rarely see him now. He's hauled me off to Wales and then prefers to spend time alone in his study."

Drinking brandy, Daniel knew.

"'Tis unfortunate he couldn't join us for our fortnight visit with the Colchesters," Daniel said aloud. "We've both known James for years through our London acquaintances."

"He said he might be able to come for the last few days. He's a busy man, you know."

"Aye," Daniel agreed, although from what he knew of Theodore, he was the opposite of a busy man.

Crossing his arms, he stretched out his long legs and leaned back, admiring the dramatic Welsh seascape from the window as the carriage wound along the road. He hadn't visited Wales since his youth, and his gaze wandered over the familiar footpaths leading to the sea. Everything here was the way he remembered, only better, and for the first time in years he allowed himself to relax. This was a working holiday, and he intended to enjoy the holiday part.

"Daniel?" his sister asked shortly. "You're overly engrossed with Wales. Most assuredly you've seen better views than this one."

"London is dirty and overcrowded of late. Thus, the country scenery is a welcome change."

Penelope pinched her thin lips together. "I'll ask a second time. What is your opinion of the investment property?"

"Perhaps when the bushes are pruned and the rotted wood repaired, 'twill look more like a home." Daniel chose his words carefully. He didn't want to sway them either way, for the decision was ultimately theirs. "And the inside is dark and dreary. Have you considered adding mullioned windows after your purchase?"

"We can't invest a fortune if we intend to make a profit." Penelope turned a false smile to him. "Unlike you, coin doesn't multiply in our hands as it does in yours."

He refrained from enumerating the reasons why coin didn't multiply in the Huckabee household, although they were threefold. First, Theodore's gambling had resulted in accumulated debts. Second, Theodore hadn't worked a day in his thirty years, opting to live off his father's inheritance. And third, Theodore had developed a fondness for the drink.

With feigned casualness, Daniel commented on the stunning scenery because a neat change of subject was in order.

The last thing he wanted was a discussion with Penelope about how he'd managed to double his wealth in the past six years, handling investments and meeting weekly with his solicitors. Hard work, he thought, coupled with long hours, a drive to succeed and an almighty God.

Gratefully, he lifted praise, because the Lord had blessed him, and Daniel was grateful for each and every blessing in his life. He grinned, eyeing his oftentimes difficult older sister. Even the blessing of Penelope.

After traveling over two hours, Penelope pointed to a scattering of makeshift tents and wagons near a patch of woods. "There's the Gypsy camp. I can't believe Mr. Colchester actually married a Gypsy woman. 'Tis the reason why he settled in Wales, you know."

Daniel quirked an eyebrow. "And that reason is?"

"To hide his new Gypsy wife from everyone in London. Do you realize the rumors surrounding this marriage?"

Daniel gave a heavy sigh and tapped a finger against his thigh. Ordinarily, he would've shrugged off Penelope's words, for he was well-acquainted with her judgmental character, as well as that of her husband. In fact, he wondered if the real reason why Theodore hadn't joined them was because of his prejudice toward Valentina Colchester.

In any event, Daniel refused to let Penelope's biased comment slide. Perhaps if she were confronted, she would realize the wrongness of her intolerance.

"Hide Valentina from exactly whom in London?" he challenged. "James Colchester is well-educated and a good Christian man. Besides, who wouldn't want to settle here?" He gestured toward a cottage covered in ivy surrounded by green hillsides and lush farmlands.

"Here? In this desolate country? Surely you're jesting." The look she gave him suggested he'd lost his reason.

He tried to look disinterested, managing a nonchalant

smile. On several occasions, especially of late, he had considered moving from London to a quiet, peaceful place teeming with waterfalls and lakes and mountains.

Perhaps Wales was the place he was seeking.

"English society will never accept a Gypsy," Penelope continued. "And Theodore agrees."

"I'm sure he does."

His sister fixed on him the glare he expected. To lighten the mood, he provided a broad grin. "English culture, which is so driven by the church, should take a studied look at our narrow-mindedness and read the Bible for insight."

"We do read the Bible!"

"Do we?" he asked, studying her scowl. If nothing else, he had gotten her to at least think about her narrow viewpoint. "In the end, aren't we all from the same race?"

He paused, catching sight of a woman near the Gypsy camp. She held a woven basket and was picking blueberries. His eyes widened. She stood out because of her reddish-brown hair and fair skin, so distinctive from the black-haired, olive-skinned women picking blueberries alongside her.

He leaned forward to peer out the window. Tall and slender, she wore an absurdly brightly-colored orange gown, a pink shawl draped over her shoulders. Assuredly, this beautiful woman wasn't a Gypsy. In contemplative silence, he held in a breath and just stared. Surprisingly, she resembled someone he knew from his youth.

Charity. Charity Weston.

He gripped his fingers together. Nay, it couldn't be. Charity was dead.

They'd been childhood friends, attending church together, riding their horses at a gallop through endless fields. She'd been light and skillful in the saddle, managing her horse at a breakneck speed. She'd secured her unman-

17

ageable waves into a knot, her face alive with exhilaration. Her sense of adventure outmatched even his.

He grinned, recalling their exploits. Her half-hearted attempts to play the pianoforte, plinking away with sighs of impatience, had resulted in her father declaring she didn't have a modicum of musical talent. Daniel remembered a recital performed by her and several other eleven-year-old children in a stuffy music room. Charity had forgotten her piece midway through but kept on playing, improvising with her head held high.

He'd been the first to stand and applaud when she finished, and she caught his gaze and smiled at him. She'd stood self-consciously, smoothing her ill-fitting dress and then bowing to the audience. She'd been all thin arms and skinny legs at the time.

Right then, he could've cheerfully boxed the ears of the other audience members, children, adults, and her over-bearing father, who had sniggered during her performance. In his chest, he'd felt a deep, affectionate protectiveness toward her that, at the age of fifteen, had troubled him.

The last time they'd been together was the day she reached her fourteenth birthday.

Near her home, she'd stood on her tiptoes and kissed him. He'd been startled at first, and made sure he didn't reci-procate, for she was too young. Beforehand, she'd said some-thing that had haunted his memory ever since.

Please never forget me.

He hadn't understood, assumed she referred to a time when they grew older, and married, and moved away from each other. Unquestionably, with her generously curved lips and skin as velvety as the finest cream, he knew her extraordinary beauty only needed time to develop before men would seek to court her.

In response, he'd asked her where she was going, then

turned a humorous joke to tease her. Her musical laughter resembled carillon bells. That is, when she laughed. Her smiles had become rarer as the years passed, although her mischievous nature remained intact.

And then she was gone from his life.

To clear his mind, he shook his head as the carriage curved up the drive leading to the Colchester estate.

"Whatever is the matter?" Penelope peered at him. "Are you ill? You've turned white."

He cleared his throat, still gripping his fingers together. "Do you remember a girl named Charity Weston?"

"Didn't she suddenly disappear? Her father said she died unexpectedly."

"Aye. I well remember the day of his announcement."

Daniel had taken Charity's death hard and the ache in his chest hadn't gone away for months afterward. Had she known she was going to die? Was it premonition, or a cruel fate? He prayed to God, seeking answers. God hadn't responded.

Through it all, though, he kept his faith, though he refused to believe she was gone. His heart had been too filled with feelings he could neither contain nor comprehend.

Please never forget me.

"I think I just saw her," he said quietly.

His sister drew up short. "And I think all this garden-fresh Welsh air is making you a bit mad. The girl died six years ago. Obviously, you're mistaken."

Was he? He'd seen her so clearly. He peered out the window again, gazing across the fields, although he'd lost sight of her.

He tore his gaze away. For lack of knowing what to do, what to say, he folded his arms and kept his gaze on a point above Penelope's head, focusing on the cushioned seat.

In his mind, more remembrances echoed.

Frequently, he'd been present when Charity's domineering father chastised her. A mere slip of a girl, she would face her father, undaunted, and fire a plausible explanation that sounded more like an argument. Although he'd seen her father react to her rebellion with anger, Daniel always silently applauded her courage.

"I recall very little about the girl," Penelope said, "although you spent a good deal of time with her, and she was obviously keen on you." She threw him a meaningful look.

"What's that supposed to mean?" he demanded. "She was four years younger than me." Even with the age difference, though, they'd gotten along brilliantly. She had a smile that lit his heart, a giggle so infectious, she would set him to laughter, and it would go on for hours. However, what he appreciated most about Charity was she chose honesty above all else. And her faith in God had been steadfast.

In response to his question, Penelope shrugged. "I didn't mean anything. I do know that since Charity's death, you've escorted more women to the theatre and opera than I can count. Never forming an attachment to just one woman. Although now, of course, there's Lady Lydia."

"Aye." With a reluctant nod, he agreed.

Lady Lydia was the woman his family and acquaintances expected him to wed, and a different rumor seemed to be spread every week about news of their betrothal. Somehow, he hadn't been able to make the commitment yet. Perhaps he never would.

Because at some point in his life, he stopped believing in love, sharing instead the viewpoint of many of his peers. That love was elusive, and he'd never been able to grab hold of it.

Mayhap it had happened when Charity disappeared.

Nay. He shook his head. Absolutely not.

Nonetheless, remembering the affection and love his

parents freely shared with each other made him sometimes long for that same attachment.

Their carriage stopped near the front steps of the Colchesters' stone mansion. A distinctive Welsh flag, a red dragon on a green and white background, flapped proudly in a cold rush of air. Clouds were gathering. Mayhap a storm brewed nearby.

Penelope prepared to alight, wrapping her paisley shawl around her reedy shoulders. Not one to let any subject drop without the final say, she remarked, "As for you believing you just saw Charity, what would a dead English woman be doing cavorting in Wales with a band of dirty Gypsies?"

CHAPTER 3

The following morning, Daniel awoke before dawn and spent several minutes praying. He always began and ended his days in prayer.

"Lord, guide my steps today," he said. "Help me to stand strong and choose only your ways above all others." He added a treasured Bible verse from 2 Timothy: "'For God hath not given us the spirit of fear; but of power, and of love, and of a sound mind.'"

He hoped the prayer would give him the insight he needed for the days ahead, for certainly time spent with Valentina and his sister's bias would prove challenging.

After he uttered a final amen, he washed, shaved, and cleaned his teeth. He didn't need a manservant, he decided, to pull on his white muslin shirt, striped waistcoat, and breeches. After a glance in the mirror to smooth back his unruly dark hair, he pulled on leather boots and decided to take the opportunity to explore the Colchester estate. He strode quietly down the hallway stairs whilst the rest of the household slept.

He assumed the day began for the others by eight o'clock

in the morning, because Valentina had assured them the night before that a light meal of toasted bread, jam, tea and coffee would be served at nine. He reached into his crescent pocket and pulled out his gold fob watch attached to a chain. 'Twas half past six, giving him plenty of time to explore.

He stepped outside and enthusiastically inhaled the scent of rye grass and crisp air. His stride was sure along the gritty ground as he made his way to the sea.

Dinner the previous evening had proved a sumptuous feast consisting of three courses, his favorite being chicken with mushrooms and tender leeks prepared in a butter sauce, and baked apples for dessert, all served with wine and braggot—a honeyed malt ale. Valentina and James had fulfilled their roles as host and hostess with casual grace. Fun-loving and bantering throughout the meal, they frequently gazed at each other with an affection Daniel had rarely seen between a married couple. And it had given him hope that love truly did exist.

Their son, Jeremy, James' child from his first marriage, was adorable. He hadn't spent many hours with them because, as was the custom, his nurse Elspeth put him to bed before dinner. James explained that Jeremy was deaf, and that Valentina was an attentive, loving stepmother. Daniel also learned Jeremy had had a twin sister, Beatrix, who died a few years earlier in a tragic accident.

Penelope had been careful not to insult their host's wife, although she pleaded fatigue and disappeared into her guest chamber shortly after the meal ended.

Daniel dragged his thoughts from dinner and squinted at the climbing sun. The morning air was cooler than he'd expected, and he'd left his gloves in the guest chamber. Although he started toward the sea, he changed direction and made his way toward the Gypsy camp instead. Shrugging his hands into his waistcoat pockets, he hastened his pace.

Of course, if he were truthful, this was the path he'd intended to take all along, and the reason he left the house before the rest of the household stirred. Thoughts of Charity had kept him awake much of the night, and his restless imaginings had blurred with visions of her—as a girl and as a woman.

He followed a footpath and stopped when he reached a row of blueberry bushes. He knelt and probed through the bushes, well aware a stranger would view his behavior as utterly insane. He could only imagine what Penelope would say.

Why was he chasing shadows and searching for a charming fourteen-year-old girl who no longer existed? Because, he reasoned, seeing the grown woman had aroused the same ache in his chest as when he was a young man. Charity had been his dearest friend, and losing her had filled him with an unexplainable loss.

As he straightened, a Gypsy man strode toward him from the opposite direction.

His muscles tightened. The Gypsy had come from nowhere—though how could he have missed a man dressed in buckskin breeches, a green sash about his waist, and a bright-orange scarf tied around his shiny black hair?

When the men came to stand face to face, the Gypsy's dark brows drew together in a suspicious scowl. "Are you a guest of Valentina's?" he asked.

He was tall and stood at Daniel's height.

"Aye, my sister and I arrived yesterday afternoon," Daniel replied.

"I saw your *grand* caravan when you passed the camp and went up the drive."

Did the Gypsy intend a slur when he'd emphasized the

word *grand*? Daniel let the comment pass. With a close-lipped smile, he extended his hand. "I'm Daniel Hayward."

"Luca Boldor." The Gypsy accepted his hand and they shook, but then Luca quickly dropped his hand. He looked toward the sunrise, a pure, scattered light crossing the fields. "'Tis unusual for an Englishman to rise early, aye?"

"Oftentimes I awaken at daybreak," Daniel replied.

"What brings you here?"

With supreme effort, Daniel managed to keep the emotion out of his tone. "I'm looking for someone. Yesterday, I saw a woman picking blueberries."

"Is it against the law to pick blueberries?"

"I didn't say it was."

Luca's jaw hardened. "Before you intend to cause trouble for the Roma, Valentina gave her permission for us to enjoy the Colchester land as we see fit."

"'Tis not my intention to insult you. I came this morning to see if she was still here."

"Why?" Luca let his question hang in the ensuing silence. "All the Rom women are spoken for. I suggest you find an Englishwoman." With a curt nod, he gestured toward the stone mansion.

"The woman I seek is English. Her hair is the color of copper, and her name is Charity Weston. We were ... good friends when we were young." He swallowed an unexpected lump in his throat, a sadness that refused to let go.

A muscle jerked in Luca's neck. "Were you now? Good friends with a woman in what way?"

Daniel's conscience nagged. Shouldn't he tell Luca the truth—that the woman he searched for had died? Despite his wish that she still lived, he couldn't ignore the indisputable logic that she'd been gone too long.

Telling himself he had no choice, he admitted, "We were best of friends."

Luca scrutinized him, his face becoming an unreadable blank. "There is no woman here who goes by the name of Charity," he said flatly.

"Aye, she is dead," Daniel admitted. For some reason, his heartfelt response brought a derisive gleam to Luca's eyes.

"Mayhap she is a woman dead to the English."

Daniel pondered the man's reply. And his tone, which was a suspicious mixture of amusement and disdain.

"Although somehow," Daniel whispered, half to himself, "I hoped she might still be …" He scrubbed a hand over his face. "Wishful thinking, I suppose." He turned on his heel. The pleasant vision of Charity was obviously not becoming a reality.

"Bid Valentina a good day when you see her," Luca called out as Daniel strode away.

"Aye," Daniel muttered without slowing his pace. He intended to walk back to the house and then continue on toward the sea. This had been a fool's errand, a small wish for a miracle. But only God created true miracles, his faith reminded.

He had not gone far when he heard a woman speak to Luca, asking when they would be leaving for the market.

Daniel stopped. He'd recognize her voice anywhere. He forgot everything else in the world as he pivoted.

Standing beside Luca was a beautiful woman with piercing blue eyes and hair the color of crimson. She turned from Luca to him, and for a moment the very air around them seemed to still. She sucked in a breath, then covered her mouth with her fingers. All color drained from her face.

"Charity." He reached out his arms. She was only footsteps away, and all he wanted was to embrace her, although the shock of seeing her again kept his legs paralyzed. "'Tis really you?"

"Aye." She extended her hands.

"Thank you, God," he whispered. For a moment, he closed his eyes. She was alive, and lovely, and God had brought them together in Wales.

Luca was watching them, frowning. Seeing Luca's frown, she dropped her hands and clasped them together. "What are you doing here?" she asked Daniel, shuffling backward.

"Go back to the camp." Luca's sharp command was unmistakable. "Tell the others we leave for the market as soon as I return." Quickly, he stepped between Daniel and Charity. He was obviously not caught in the same hold of paralyzing incredulity as Daniel.

"Get out of my way. I must speak with her." Daniel recovered from the surprise of seeing her and attempted to thrust Luca aside. He was met with a furious glare as the Gypsy stood firm. Slowly, Luca pushed up the sleeves of his muslin shirt.

A clash with Luca was the last thing he wanted, Daniel thought, as he frantically reviewed the alternatives.

"Shall we let the lady decide?" he asked. He peered past Luca and fixed his gaze on Charity. Appealing. Praying. Hoping.

"Daniel, please ..." Her eyes met his, and she lifted her hands palms up, a plea for understanding. "I can't."

"Don't you remember all the days we spent together?"

Did she know how long he'd grieved when she'd disappeared?

"I'm sorry." Her gaze softened, her expression yielding. And it was for him, he knew it was. Now if only Luca would permit them to speak alone.

Daniel studied the man, sizing him up, weighing the probable outcome of a skirmish. Perhaps it was the best way to settle this. Luca, meanwhile, was helping himself to a handful of blueberries, taking his time, keeping himself between Daniel and Charity. The disdainful look on his face banished the last of Daniel's patience.

Anger surged as he firmly shoved Luca aside and strode forward.

"Charity, you disappeared on me once, and 'twill not happen again." He reached her and firmly put his hands on her shoulders. She squirmed, although she didn't move away. "All this time, your father said you were dead."

At the mention of her father, her blue eyes iced up, and her entire demeanor changed. Gone was the yielding smile, the warmth in her gaze.

"I am very much alive and will speak plainly." Her spine stiffened as she stood straight and faced him squarely. "Please don't come here again. I am dead to anyone from my past."

Then she twisted free and ran toward the Gypsy camp.

CHAPTER 4

*D*aniel Hayward. It couldn't be.

In the solitude of her tent, Charity sank onto the wooden bench. Her skin was still tingling, her hands shaking from their encounter. She cried off going to the marketplace, knowing Luca wasn't pleased with her decision. However, it couldn't be helped.

As if she had last seen him on the previous day, she mulled over the years she'd spent with him. Aye, she dreamed about him more often than she admitted.

And then he had appeared from her dreams to reality—his eyes the same entrancing silver-grey, his muscular frame filled out with the promise she'd seen in the young man. His deep voice when he'd called her name was achingly recognizable. Instinctively, she'd extended both hands to him before seeing Luca's furious expression.

Why would Daniel be in Wales, of all places? Mayhap he knew Mr. Colchester, because wealthy gentlemen were well-acquainted with each other in their exclusive London circles. She recalled Luca mentioning Mr. Colchester had investments in London, although he conducted most business from Wales.

Very likely that was the connection, she mused. Daniel had always been interested in finance and had excelled in math studies. Unlike herself. She held a smile. How often had he helped her when she couldn't make sense of the formal columns of numbers, despite her tutor?

Or, she reasoned, there was a chance it could all be a mere coincidence he was here.

Satisfied with her rationalization, she swung around and gathered the basket of blueberries she'd picked the day before, intending to cook them over the outdoor fire. If sugar was brought back from the market, she could add a glaze. 'Twas better, she reasoned, if she kept her mind and hands busy.

Before she reached the opening of her tent, she stopped in midstep. Her feverishly working brain had offered up another, more pressing reason why Daniel was in Wales. She set down the basket and caught her breath.

Assuming her father had been looking for her all these years, could he have somehow made the connection between Mr. Colchester and the Gypsies? Could he have found out she'd joined a Gypsy tribe after she ran away? And then, because her father knew she trusted Daniel, could he have asked the boy who used to be her friend to come for her and bring her back to England?

Nay. She contemplated the logic with a sinking heart before dismissing it. Daniel would never betray her, because friends didn't betray each other, did they? And although she'd never spoken of her father's abuse aloud, surely Daniel had detected the pain in her voice, the anguish in her movements whenever it was time for her to leave his house and a servant escorted her home.

Despite her attempts to keep the remembrances at bay,

her father's biting comments regarding her lack of musical skill, her unladylike antics as she climbed trees or used a slingshot, bubbled to the surface. She'd been a great disappointment to him.

And then she remembered the time she'd spent in Daniel and Penelope's home. Their parents were loving and kind toward each other, their interest in their children genuine and unmistakable. She had longed to live in Daniel's house, to spend her days in an atmosphere of harmony and tranquility, following God with a tenacious faith that had abandoned her long ago.

She sighed. She'd always regarded Daniel as her blessing from God, her guardian angel who cheered her days despite her unbearable home life. And she had missed him, missed seeing him. Certainly, it wouldn't hurt to speak with him one last time. Indeed, there was no harm in conversing with an old friend.

Making up her mind, she glanced at herself in the small mirror beside her washbasin. She splashed cool water on her face, changed into a jaunty yellow gown and tucked her corkscrew curls into a makeshift bun tied with a yellow ribbon. With her chin lifted in resolve, she opened her tent, breathed in a lungful of fresh country air and stepped outside. The camp was quiet, as most of her tribesmen had accompanied Luca to the market in town. Some remained, giving her a brief nod before returning to their chores.

Kezia, stout and bent over with age, stood over a pot on the campfire stirring soup. The air around her was thick with the pungent scents of black pepper and garlic.

"You look exceptionally lovely, Charani." The dark lines in Kezia's face told the story of a harsh outdoor life.

"Thank you." Intending to keep her pace brisk, Charity continued walking.

"Shuk tski khalpe la royasa," Kezia said. She placed the

31

spoon beside the soup on a wooden bowl, then picked up her sewing, which was never far from her side. Today, she was mending holes in a pile of brightly colored blankets.

"Aye." *Beauty cannot be eaten with a spoon*, Charity silently translated, and nodded in response. But what exactly did that mean? Wasn't a woman allowed to fuss with her appearance once in a while? Or did it mean something else? She didn't dare ask, for Kezia was known to talk nonstop if the subject interested her.

"Where are you going?"

Charity had made it to the edge of the camp and turned back to Kezia. "I'm going for a walk."

The old woman retied the bright scarf around her snowy-white hair. "Which path are you taking? I prefer the path to the sea—except all that sand and some of the rocks are slippery. However, a hike up one of the many mountains in this country might be preferable, although then the rocks are the size of boulders and difficult to get around. I prefer—"

"Thank you, Kezia. I have a certain destination in mind, so I know which path to take. Mayhap we can chat later, by the campfire."

Determined to end the discussion, Charity turned and hastened her steps. Even as the camp grew farther away, she still heard Kezia's voice instructing her about path preferences.

A smile drifted across Charity's lips. Kezia was a good woman and beloved by the entire tribe. If she enjoyed chatting, then she'd certainly earned the right.

Tipping her head up, she shaded her eyes and peered at the sun. Years ago, she and Daniel had agreed they favored riding in the afternoon, when the weather was warm. So, she'd check the Colchesters' stables first.

Daniel, she thought, wiping her cold clammy hands along her gown. *I'm coming.*

* * *

THE STABLES WERE SURROUNDED by a white-painted fence. Beyond them, a path led to steep mountain ranges. Wales was a country of rare beauty, for another path led to the rough sea and a beach mostly made up of stones and rocks.

As she approached the stable, she appreciatively stroked the glossy neck of a chestnut horse standing at the fence. "You're magnificent, aren't you? I expect you're one of Valentina's favorites."

A groom came out from around the fence and introduced himself as Andrew. He was short and thin, his hair greying at the temples. "Are you Mr. Haywood's sister?" he asked.

Charity chuckled. "Nay, I'm—"

"Charity?" Daniel stepped from the stable, a riding crop tucked beneath his arm. "I heard your voice ... I thought I might be imagining ..." He looked around, his gaze narrowed. "Is your Gypsy guardian hiding behind a blueberry bush, impatient to pick a fight with me?"

"Luca?" She laughed and shook her head. "He's not my guardian. He's just a little overprotective of his women."

"A little?" Daniel flashed her a look and then frowned. His grip on the crop tightened. "Are you one of his women?"

She met his gaze, which had gone from warm to cold. "Of course not. Gypsies don't have harems or anything like that. They marry one person."

"So the man is married."

"Nay. He doesn't have time and he's more interested in keeping the tribe alive than any one woman."

"Aye, except he is a man and—" He seemed to want to say more, but paused and thought better of it. He handed Andrew his crop and Andrew stepped back into the stable. Coolness was still in his gaze when he turned back to her. "Then why are you here, Charity?"

"I remembered you used to go riding at this time of day ... I mean, we went riding ..."

"Congratulations for at least remembering something about us," he said impersonally.

She realized she was staring at him and, despite his coolness, felt herself melt a little. He was so handsome, even more handsome than she remembered. She passed an admiring glance over his flawless white shirt, open at the collar, and blue riding jacket. Black breeches and leather boots hugged his strong legs, and she couldn't help noting the tiny crinkles around his eyes.

Six years, Daniel, she reflected, and held in a breath. She'd carried off a cool outer bravery with the Gypsies, but had also bottled up excess emotion. Now, looking at him, she choked back tears for all the time they had lost because of her impulsiveness ... because of her desperation to get away from her father.

A breeze ruffled his deep-brown hair, the color of dark chocolate, and she imagined running her fingers through the thickness.

Nay, she told herself.

But another voice answered, *you know you want to.*

She averted her gaze, afraid he'd see the longing in her eyes.

"We think alike, we always did," he said. "When I came to the stables earlier today, I thought of you. Then when I saw how splendid the horses are, I knew you would love them as much as I did." She looked up as he walked toward her, interest replacing the earlier coolness in his expression. "Are you here because you want to go riding?"

"I hadn't intended to ride."

"And yet here you are at the stables." His eyes sparkled with challenge. "You haven't forgotten how to ride and race, have you?"

She drew herself up straight. "I've ridden ever since I was a young girl. You know that."

"Well, you've obviously been around the Gypsies a long while. Mayhap you're out of practice." He gestured toward the stable, grinning. "You can choose a tame horse. Perhaps Old Biscuit. He's quiet and agreeable, and you'll enjoy a merry promenade whilst he sniffs the rosebushes every few feet. I promise I'll give you a head start."

"Your memory is apparently faulty." Her lips twitched with laughter. "I used to beat *you* when we raced."

"Did I declare a race? If so, I probably should share my secret with you." He shrugged, then looked away. "I meant to tell you a long time ago."

She plunked her hands on her hips. "And that secret is …?"

"Oftentimes I let you win because 'twas the gentlemanly thing to do."

"You didn't let me win. I beat you!" She took a step forward, intending to pass him and walk into the stable to choose her horse. "If anything, you cheated."

"Me?" He beamed a charming smile, his white teeth gleaming. "A Christian man?"

"You always were impossible, and now you're using Christianity as an excuse." She attempted to render him a stern glare, although her shoulders spoiled her efforts by shaking with laughter.

"So 'tis agreed? We'll ride together, just as we used to."

Aye, just as they'd done years ago, although everything was different now.

He was quiet, apparently awaiting her reply. When she didn't speak, he said her name and touched her shoulder lightly. Her heart did an unexpected flip in her chest as uncertainty collided with want. Debating, she fixed her gaze on the row of boxwood hedges lining the edge of the fencing.

Considering Daniel's teasing tone and the fact she hadn't had the opportunity to ride for pleasure in many years, she took the bait and agreed. Or mayhap 'twas because of the way her pulse raced whenever she looked at him.

Nay. Certainly not.

In any event, she quashed her feelings and justified that time spent with him was the surest way to discover if he was a spy sent by her father.

Daniel's steps were sure as he strode beside her into the coolness of the stables. He'd grown a couple of inches and now stood half a head taller than she, still lean and splendidly fit. As he showed her around, one part of her wanted to throw her arms around him and breathe in the warm masculine smells of worn leather and fresh air. The other part wanted to stand back and reproach him for suddenly appearing in Wales and setting her emotions in turmoil.

After admiring the horses, she chose a magnificent sturdy bay. The horse poked its nose through the stall and nuzzled her hand.

"Will he do?" Daniel asked. "His name is Chester."

She stroked the horse's black mane. "Aye, Chester is perfect."

The groom saddled the horse and led Chester outdoors to the mounting block, where Daniel assisted her onto the sidesaddle.

"Will you ride Old Biscuit?" she couldn't resist teasing. "Or maybe Twinkle Feet?"

He laughed out loud. "My horse's name is Bandit. He's the one I rode this morning and he will do nicely." He nodded to a black stallion being led out of the stable by Andrew. After swinging up onto the horse's back, he drew his horse abreast to hers and then took the lead. She guided her horse and followed Daniel to a quiet corner of the pasture.

She viewed the golden sun streaming through the leaves of the trees. "Now that you've brought me here, shall we wait until twilight to ride or is there something I'm missing?"

"I wanted a moment to be sure you were real—that this moment is real. I wanted to take the time to appreciate it."

She smiled at him, at his honesty. He always had the ability to speak his mind.

Once, when she asked how he always seemed so sure of himself, he told her it wasn't him. He relied on God's grace to keep him steady. More than anything, she was starting to believe that it was through God's goodness that they had been reunited.

He nodded, apparently thinking the same. He had also always had the ability to read her thoughts.

Vaguely, she took in the sights of a splendid summer afternoon. Squirrels skittered up and over tree branches, a group of plump pheasants wandered nearby. Unable to stifle her contented sigh, she savored the peace enveloping her heart. It had been a long time since she'd felt so serene.

"Dare I suppose your smile indicates a softening of your initial reaction toward me?" he asked. "In the blueberry patch, you didn't seem at all pleased."

"You're mistaken," she lied. "I've never had a reaction to you one way or the other."

She knew her cheeks had colored. Whenever she was around him, she struggled to hide her innermost feelings to no avail, thanks to her fair, telltale complexion.

He guided his horse nearer and ran his hand along hers. "On the contrary, I think you have a strong reaction to me, as I have to you." Very quickly, very lightly, he leaned over and pressed a kiss on her temple.

She fixed her gaze on the pheasants, not him. Reflexively, her fingers tightened around her reins.

"Charity. Look at me."

She took judicious note of the tenderness in his tone as she met his gaze. Slowly, he bent his head. She knew he was going to kiss her.

"Are you set then, Mr. Haywood, Miss ...?" Andrew shouted from the stable. She picked out his thin form as he gestured toward them.

"Her surname is Weston," Daniel called back, then returned his gaze to her. "I assume you're not married, Charity. Or is there a Gypsy man who's interested in you?"

"There is one. His name is Petshah, although he is old and cranky, and always looks tired because of his heavy eyelids. When we met, I couldn't tell if he was sleeping or awake."

His expression darkened. "Has he woken up enough to declare himself?"

She shook her head. "Not yet." And if Petshah ever did, she'd run as hard and as fast as she could to avoid him, despite Luca's apparent approval.

She hesitated before asking Daniel, "And you?"

"The right woman has eluded me."

Until now.

He hadn't said the words, yet she heard them in the silence just the same.

She tried to think of a quick rejoinder, but he'd already swiveled in the saddle. "Ready?"

"We're racing? Now?" She took a moment to digest this, to calm the steady pounding of her heart and then tighten the yellow ribbon around her hair. "How much of a warning will you give me?"

"None! I cheat, remember? First one to reach the stone wall wins." He pointed to a wall a good distance ahead of them. With a laugh, he broke into a showy trot, then full gallop.

38

He didn't give her a choice. Chester tossed his head, impatient to join the race.

She leaned forward. "C'mon, let's beat them!" With a joyous laugh, she galloped after Daniel.

CHAPTER 5

*W*hen Daniel glanced over his shoulder, apparently gauging his lead, she estimated he was five lengths ahead of her. Her horse's hooves thundered over the hard ground as Chester strove to close the distance. Quickly, she gained back the five lengths and assumed she'd reach the stone wall first. At the last second, Daniel's horse edged past hers and won by scarcely a hairsbreadth.

She laughed, exhilarated by the hard ride. Refreshing breezes cooled her cheeks and revived her spirits, and she felt more animated than she had felt in years.

"I've always loved to ride horses," she said as she slowed Chester. "The faster, the better."

"And I've always loved the privilege of watching you ride at full speed, although my heart was often in my throat."

"Then and now?"

"Aye."

"Whatever for?"

"I was fearful you were sometimes too careless, despite the obstacles." He grinned when she frowned and held up a hand. "Sometimes. I said *sometimes* and please take it as a compliment. Even when you were twelve, you were an expert horsewoman." He swung down from his horse, assisted her dismount, then tied their horses' reins to a birch tree. On the far side of the stone wall, a meadow led to a burbling stream. Skylarks twittered from the trees.

"May I remind you I won our race today?" Daniel asked triumphantly, tickling her under the chin.

"May I remind *you* that you cheated? If I'd had a five-second lead like you had, I would've easily beat you."

"We'll have a rematch come the morrow. Your riding skill against mine."

Motivated by the challenging flicker in his eyes, she took up the gauntlet and agreed, soundly warning him not to cheat again. Only afterward did she realize he had success-fully maneuvered her into seeing him again.

"If I am with you," he said, "than I'm the obvious winner, no matter how fast you ride."

She regarded his boyish grin. Despite his joking, she again heard the tenderness in his voice, saw it in his gaze.

"If we walk to the stream," he said, his tone casual, "we'll have a view of the entire estate."

He took her hand, and they strolled through a fragrant meadow blooming with wildflowers and tall grass, until they found the pathway to the stream. She blew back a wisp of hair that had fallen onto her face. As they climbed, she retied the yellow ribbon holding back her unruly ringlets.

When they reached the stream, he shrugged off his jacket and spread it on the bank. Standing beside him, she gazed at the splendid view of the Colchester grounds, unmatched by any she'd ever seen in England. In Wales, the landscape was forever wild and untamed.

Daniel pointed out a garden in the distance, explaining it was Valentina's herb garden. There, he explained, Valentina tended plants used for healing sicknesses—dandelion root and flaxseed and coriander. Because Kezia used many of these same plants, Charity was familiar with the herbs' benefits.

"Shall we rest here a while?" he asked.

She nodded. Having his strong hand clasped warmly around hers brought a gentle, jubilant harmony to her heart.

Whispers of their youth—chaperoned picnics by a lake as smooth as glass while they watched a group of swans gliding past, the sun warming their faces, the varying shades of wild-flowers when he picked her bouquets. All these memories were so joyful.

Although, she reminded herself, she hadn't yet confronted him about her father. But then she shook her head. Not today. The afternoon was too perfect for such unpleasantness. Besides, it wasn't in her nature to be churlish and blame Daniel for a suspicion that might not be true.

He was watching her, and she wondered whether she should stand or sit. She opted for letting go of his hand and sitting on his jacket.

To break the silence, she remarked on the stretch of good weather as she settled her gown around her. She went on, explaining how she planned to boil the blueberries she'd picked with a sugar glaze when she returned to camp.

He listened without interrupting. When she finished, she glanced up at him. Her subject matter had seemed to amuse him for he was grinning.

"So you believe you'll beat me come the morrow, aye?" he teased, gazing upward. Wispy clouds floated across a gloriously blue sky. "Even if it rains?"

She grinned. "I can beat you in a downpour if I rode a chicken."

He chuckled and sat beside her. "In all the years I've known you, I've always found our conversations so …" He paused, seeming to grasp for the words. "So joyful."

She grinned at his choice of the word *joyful,* the same word she'd thought a few moments earlier.

"How long have we known each other?" she asked. "It seems like we've been best friends my entire life."

"I remember the first time I saw you. Our families had known each other for a while, and we were sharing a mutual tutor. When you left the tutor's house, you put on an absurd hat that seemed to have foxgloves growing out of it." He sat back and propped his shoulders against a thick tree trunk. "I recall you and your father arguing about that hat because he insisted you wear it."

"That sounds like our relationship."

She reflected on the day when she first realized Daniel was her champion. It had started that day. He'd paused to speak with her father, discussing finance with the knowledge of a forty-year-old seasoned investor. She'd yanked off the hat and hid it behind the tutor's boxwood hedges. After her father had finished his discussion with Daniel, they'd left the tutor's house and departed for home. And her father had forgotten all about the hat.

His gaze shifted from her face to her hair. "I still remember that hat. You looked lovely."

"I looked anything but lovely." She waved her hands dismissively. "However, you saved me from wearing a silly purple confection and I was eternally grateful. Did you know foxgloves can grow to over six feet tall?"

"Aye, and I feared they were actually starting to sprout, so I had no choice but to come to your rescue." His gaze slid meaningfully to her lips, and the obvious interest in his grey eyes was clear. "I don't believe you ever thanked me for saving you from that hat."

Instinctively, she scooted back. "Of course I did." Under different circumstances, she might have laughed. However, sitting so close to him, feeling the warmth of his breath brushing against her cheeks, tender memories made her want him as strongly as he obviously wanted her.

Nay, she told herself. *You're no longer an adolescent girl with a crush on a handsome man.* She was now a grown woman who'd lived among the Gypsies for six years. However, that didn't mean she was experienced around men. Although Luca was her friend, most of the men in her tribe were elderly. And Petshah, the man Luca had suggested for her, was a giant of a man, balding, with a mouthful of teeth resembling a picket fence.

She situated her gown primly around her legs and sat up straighter.

If she thought that would deter Daniel, she was mistaken. He whispered her name, a smile lurking in his voice, and then, without warning, his lips gently descended on hers. She kissed him back, yielding to her desire to be closer to him. When he lifted his mouth, she was trembling.

He drew her closer. His lips brushed against her temple while his gaze canvassed the landscape. "'Twill be time for dinner soon," he said. "'Tis time we leave."

For some reason, she wanted to finish their conversation, to start taking down the barrier she'd erected between them.

"When you saw my father and me at the tutor's house," she said softly, "he was merely doing what he always did— attempting to browbeat me into becoming a proper English lady."

Daniel's gaze narrowed. He drew back his head and studied her face. "You mean he used force?"

"Aye." She winced, remembering. "And I resisted."

"Charity." Caringly, he cupped her face in his hands. "*Force* and *resisted* are two words that alarm me, especially when they concern you. Tell me what happened."

He deserved an explanation, although she was ashamed of

the way her father had treated her. And then she had done a very un-Christian-like thing and run away from home.

He tipped up her chin. "Why did you leave? Your father said you were dead."

A flush crept up her cheeks. "You could never understand. Your life at home was so different from mine."

"Try me anyway."

For an interminable moment, she hesitated, then met his sympathetic gaze straight on.

"My father was cruel. I don't know why. Mayhap he didn't love me." She caught the sob before it welled in her throat. "Mayhap he was resentful."

"Why? You were his only child—his only family."

"And I was a girl, not an heir. To add to the wound, my mother died birthing me."

"Surely you don't blame yourself for her death."

She gazed up at him, amazed again that he was sitting beside her, so handsome and so caring. "I don't know what I believe and don't believe. My faith in God is no longer strong, either."

"God is just and always with us."

"Mayhap with your family. He certainly wasn't anywhere near mine." She stretched out her legs.

Although still watching her intently, he dropped his hand.

"Your family prayed often, displaying their faith publicly," she said. "When I dined at your house, I remember bowing my head and I even remember the blessing." She took a deep breath. "'Lord,'" she began, "'thank you for the food set in front of us, the loved ones sitting beside us, and the love we have for each other. Amen.'" As she recited the simple verse, Daniel joined in with her.

She sighed. "'Twas wonderful, the feeling of belonging in a loving household."

45

"Faith is meant to be more than a supper blessing, more than a feeling."

"What is faith, then?" She tilted her head back to regard him. "I don't understand."

"Faith is difficult, yet easy to explain." He leaned back on his forearms. "You can examine faith forever and have endless discussions about it, but you don't have to be exultant or even appreciative to have faith. Faith simply means that whatever the storm, you're going to get through it."

His words hung significantly in the stillness.

She studied him. He had turned his head to gaze at a red deer in the woodlands. The deer stood majestic and at frozen attention, staring back at them.

"Do you remember any Bible passages?" Daniel asked.

"I recited multitudes of Bible passages as I knelt on a cold stone floor when I was being punished for acting unladylike, or whatever the transgression my father chose to accuse me of that day." She shivered, recalling the heavy closet door falling shut behind her, latching into place as her father locked her into the dark linen closet for hours.

Sadness and regret shadowed Daniel's eyes. "Charity, I didn't know. Why didn't you tell me?" He shook his head. "I should've known," he whispered.

"How? I certainly never told you." She drew in a shaking breath. "Whenever you asked if anything was the matter, I'd accord you a brief dismissal. You weren't a seer."

"But I knew you. And, deep in my gut, I knew something was wrong." He pulled her to his chest and gathered her close. "I'm sorry. I'm so, so sorry. I should have protected you. I always vowed to myself that I would keep you safe."

She placed her hand on his chest. His heart beat warm and strong and alive.

"None of this was your fault," she said. "Truly, you were the anchor safeguarding my days and your kindness empowered me to get through my sorrowful nights. I wish I had my faith to lean on, as you have yours. But 'tis too late. I have too many doubts now."

"'Tis where you are misguided." He took her hands in his and gently squeezed. "Having doubts doesn't mean you don't have faith. Faith is the conviction that God is real. You remember Hebrews 11:1?"

"Aye. 'Now faith is the substance of things hoped for, the evidence of things not seen.'"

"And you, my beautiful Charity, are most assuredly a woman of God."

His words were directed straight to her heart.

"Sometimes I long to return to church," she said. "I hear church bells ring out from whatever towns we're camped near on Sunday mornings. Not long ago, I sat outside one of the churches to listen to the service."

"Would you come with me to church on Sunday?"

She took a deep breath, watching the shy hares hopping through the grass, this way and that, as if they weren't sure where they were going.

"I would like to attend with you," she finally said.

"Good."

She gave him her full attention. "Luca might not approve … Although I think you'll like him once you get to know him. And the tribe … Everyone is so fun-loving, good-hearted and—"

"I can hardly wait to meet them and pray they're more hospitable than Luca." Daniel's long fingers moved up her arm in a delightful caress. "Although if someone told me I'd be visiting a Gypsy camp after I arrived in Wales, I would've assured them they were mad."

She grinned. "And now?"

He bent his head, and a flurry of nervousness rose from her belly.

"Daniel, I—"

He pressed his forefinger to her lips, halting her words. "And now I believe 'tis high time you thank me for saving you from wearing an outrageous hat. So, I'll accept your gratitude now." With that, he took his time and tenderly kissed her.

When he released her, she snuggled her head against his shoulder. "When I came to see you, this was not how I envisioned our encounter was supposed to go today."

"'Tis exactly the way it should've gone. 'Tis perfect." He kissed her again, his mouth firm and sweet. "Charity, I've missed you so much."

After the kiss ended, he assisted her to her feet, brushed the leaves off his jacket, and wrapped it around her. Taking her hand, he led her back through the meadow where the horses waited. Sunlight bathed the fields, lighting everything in its path. For a moment, it seemed that heaven and earth touched.

Her eyes brimmed with tears, although these were grateful tears. The day had dawned, the afternoon complete as they rode back to the stables.

And Daniel Hayward was at her side.

Just as he'd always been.

As if she had never left.

CHAPTER 6

*I*n her tent, Charity sat on the wooden stool by her washbasin and critically appraised herself in her hand mirror. She combed her burnished-copper locks into a low bun and tied a lavender-colored velvet ribbon around them. Her dark-purple gown with flowing bell sleeves fit her to perfection. Encouraged by Kezia, she had purchased the fabric at the village market. Kezia had sketched the garment, then her nimble fingers had gone to work as she sewed the gown to Charity's measurements.

It had hung in Charity's tent for several days, sending a trill of excitement through her pulse every time she beheld it. For 'twas the gown she planned to wear to a formal dinner at Valentina and James Colchester's house.

Standing up, she turned and Kezia fastened the back buttons of the gown. Then she twirled. The gown, tight-fitting at the waist and widening at the hem, cast gay whirling shadows across the canvas tent. She fingered the diamond necklace at her throat, a gift sent earlier in the day from Valentina and delivered by a footman, and watched it shimmer in the candlelight. Tiny matching earrings completed the effect. Once again, she was a regal English lady.

Kezia clasped her hands together and took a step back to survey Charity's appearance. "You are the most dazzling princess I've ever seen, Charity," she declared.

Of late, Charity had overheard the Gypsy men murmuring that she was comely, despite her fair skin and red hair, and she smiled. Finally, she'd been accepted, at least somewhere.

"Thank you." She acknowledged Kezia's compliment with a smile. "Although I'm far from a princess ..." Pausing, she grasped Kezia's shoulders. "Wait a minute. You haven't called me by my English name since I arrived. Why now?"

"Because the tribe is traveling south and I won't see you anymore." Kezia patted Charity's back with her small hand. "And because you're taking a new step—away from the Rom —and toward the future where you truly belong."

Charity leaned back to regard the elderly woman. Kezia stared back, her dark gaze dancing beneath thinly arched eyebrows. As much as her mind denied Kezia's words, her heart said otherwise.

"I'm both excited and nervous about tonight," she admitted. "Does that make sense?"

"Perfect sense." Kezia stood on her toes and pressed her rough cheek against Charity's smooth one. Her wise voice whispered Romany words Charity didn't understand, but she knew they were meant to encourage and embolden her.

A fortnight had passed so quickly, Charity reflected, and come the morrow Daniel and Penelope were leaving the Colchester estate to return to Penelope's summer house that she'd rented in Wales.

Since the first day she'd chanced upon Daniel at the blueberry bushes, they'd ridden their horses at breakneck speed, watched incredible sunny days pass, and, most important, shared memories. They stole away every hour they could, kissing by a secluded pond, lingering over lavish picnic spreads the Colchester servants served—cold chicken and sliced ham and buttered biscuits one day, bread pudding and pigeon pie the next.

Despite her frequent inward rebuttals, she knew she was falling in love with him, just as she had when she was a girl. It was against her better sense, of course, for a wealthy man's future didn't lie with a woman who'd become a Gypsy and therefore had nothing to offer—no dowry, no fancy London lifestyle, and a decided lack of ladylike mannerisms. Yet when they spoke gaily of shared reminiscences, or had spirited discussions about God, her heart refused to listen to her logical mind.

She soon learned that Daniel's mathematical intellect was as brilliant as ever, and his wise London investments frequently paid off handsomely. He was remarkably perceptive, balancing his knowledge with sensible ventures, and he had accumulated wealthy reserves in just a few years. One day he casually mentioned he didn't need to work in London anymore, and had considered purchasing property in Wales.

It was the first time he'd brought up the subject of a future, and she carefully sidestepped the discussion. Besides, she hadn't confronted him about possibly working with her father to bring her home, and she'd vowed never to return to the life she once led.

Two nights before Daniel was slated to leave, Luca greeted the news that she was dining at the Colchester home with as much enthusiasm as if he'd been told she planned to dine with highwaymen.

"I thought you wanted me to dine and converse with the English," she countered. "Daniel's sister, Penelope, is staying with the Colchester's, and I distinctly recall you telling me that English company would be good for me. Something about bringing back the pink color in my cheeks."

"Did I, indeed?" He quirked a dark eyebrow. "I don't remember."

She burst out laughing. Typical male, remembering only what was convenient.

"And since when do you listen to anything I say, anyway?" he continued.

"I'm here, aren't I?" She plunked her hands on her hips. "I traveled with your tribe all the way from England, and that trip took months because of all the rain and mud."

"A minor detail." He shrugged, and she couldn't tell if he was joking or serious.

Kezia, however, made no secret about wanting to meet Daniel.

"He's Charity's young man," she boasted to the tribesmen one evening as they shared a meal around the campfire. Pivoting to Charity, she predicted, "I guarantee you'll wed him by summer's end. We will be gone by then, so be sure to tell him he must jump over a broom with you. 'Tis a Romany wedding tradition and good luck."

Charity had refuted Kezia's prediction, though she smiled at the broom reference. Because Romany weddings were not recognized by the church, they were forced to marry through nonchurch rituals. A broomstick ceremony involved the couple jumping over a broom placed in the doorway to a home, signifying sweeping away the old life and jumping into the new.

Now, seeing Kezia's bright smile, Charity knew this past fortnight, lighthearted and joyous, was the beginning of something that was hard to put into words. Or mayhap she didn't want to put it into words, for fear her happiness would disappear.

During the hours she and Daniel spent apart, she missed

him, then felt foolish for missing him. She'd been without him for many years. Why would their reunion make her want to see him more, not less?

Kezia poked her head outside the tent. "He should be arriving soon, aye?" she said gaily, another prediction.

Charity sent her a reassuring smile. "Aye."

Moments later, both women turned at the clip-clop of horses' hooves.

"He's early." With a smug smile, Kezia held out her hand. "He obviously can't wait to see you and a lady never keeps a gentleman waiting. Come."

Although the Gypsy camp was less than a mile from the main house, Daniel had insisted on borrowing a carriage from the Colchesters so Charity wouldn't have to walk.

She snatched a paisley shawl to wrap around her shoulders. Hand in hand, she and Kezia stepped from her tent and walked toward the carriage, elegant and lacquered a gleaming moss-green. The hood of the carriage was raised, and two midnight-black horses tossed their heads and whinnied.

Daniel stepped down from the carriage. Carrying a bouquet of wildflowers, he hastened to meet her halfway. When they stopped, face-to-face and a foot apart, he cast a puzzled glance at the tribesmen surrounding them.

Charity sent him a reassuring smile. "This is my dear friend Kezia," she said.

"I've heard a lot about you." Daniel turned a genuine smile to the woman.

"And I about you, young man." Her thick lips wreathed in a smile, Kezia dropped Charity's hand and stepped to the side.

"You look beautiful tonight, Charity." He came nearer, and his gaze smoldered as he regarded her. "And you've achieved something quite remarkable."

"Something remarkable?" she repeated.

"Aye, my love." He closed the distance between them. "You're even more gorgeous than when you were fourteen."

She felt the warm flare of color in her cheeks. He'd never called her *my love* before.

He handed the fragrant flowers to her. "These are for you."

"Thank you." She smiled and sniffed them—the scent of greenery and sweetness, reminding her of days spent with him that she had cherished in her heart.

"Just like old times, aye? Oftentimes in the past, I traipsed through many a meadow to pick you a bouquet after you told me you loved wildflowers."

She said nothing, for what could she say? She was caught in the enchantment of his captivating eyes, the wonderful memories his tender voice evoked.

He shifted closer, bending his head.

Just behind her, Luca cleared his throat. Kezia, speaking in a voice loud enough for everyone to hear, declared, "*Kon del tut o nai shai dela tut wi o vast.*"

Charity stifled a laugh.

At Daniel's look of perplexity, she translated, "It means, 'He who willingly gives you one finger will also give the whole hand.'" She added, whispering in his ear, "Although I may not be exactly correct. When it comes to Romany sayings, I'm never sure."

"I understand the significance of the words." He pulled her to him and she squirmed, knowing they were in full view of her tribesmen. "It means, I will give you anything in my possession, whether big or small. And I willingly give you my heart." He spoke quietly, with deep emotion. He was a man who wasn't ashamed to show his feelings. He was a man who would always protect her.

Although Luca and Daniel had previously met, their

greetings were stilted. Luca deliberately used Charity's Gypsy name, Charani, rather than her English name.

Other tribesmen followed suit with overformal introductions, keeping a respectable distance and eyeing Daniel, whom they considered a *gadje*, with suspicious interest.

For the first time, she noticed that several of the wagons had been packed and numerous tents were down.

At her quizzical glance, Luca shrugged and replied, "We'll be traveling again soon."

She realized Kezia had said the same thing in her tent, as she helped Charity dress. She hadn't put much weight on her words. "I thought you liked it here," she said to Luca.

"We are a wanderlust people, Charani. You know that."

Daniel interrupted, saying that they needed to go. She handed the flowers to Kezia for safekeeping, and then Daniel assisted her into the carriage. She felt the solidity of him as he settled on the seat beside her. Her gaze wandered sidewise, appreciating his good looks—strong legs clad in shiny leather boots and sandy brown breeches, a buttoned white muslin shirt, and brick-colored waistcoat.

With a contented sigh, she leaned back against the velvet seat. In the deepening dusk of a glorious August evening, she gazed at the tranquil night sky.

"What's a *gadje*?" Daniel asked, as he gave the lively horses the prompt to start.

Her gaze shot toward him. "Why do you ask?"

"Because I overheard Luca and the other men talking and assumed they were referring to me."

"'Tis a Romany word. It means you aren't one of them. In your case, 'tis because you're English. As am I."

"So, you're a gadje, also."

"Aye, although when I mentioned this fact to Luca, he stated most emphatically that because I've lived in the tribe so long and adopted to the Gypsy ways, I'm not considered a gadje anymore."

"So, a gadje is an insult?"

"Aye, most assuredly. And when I reminded him I didn't believe in spirits, Luca stated that being a gadje was about more than religion. 'Twas a mindset and way of life. I didn't agree with his observation but thought it best not to tell him."

"And your Gypsy name ... is Charani? That explains why Luca feigned ignorance when I asked him about a woman named Charity." He shook his head. "Convenient."

"He was only trying to protect me." At Daniel's frosty glare, she groped for a safer subject. She wished Luca hadn't used her Gypsy name so noticeably.

"Charani is a Gypsy name and it means bird," she added.

"Really? Then you are a bird? A bird who prefers to fly away?"

She hesitated. She didn't want their last evening together to be spoiled by something as unimportant as a name. Desperately seeking their earlier pleasantries, she remarked, "Thank you for taking me to church services on Sunday."

"My pleasure." His glance met hers, along with a grin that all was forgiven. "The vicar's sermon was one of encouragement and faith."

"And wisdom. I appreciated when he said everything that happens in our lives—all the bad, all the pain—enables us to fully appreciate the good."

"Aye." He urged the horses into a trot. "Although we can't see around a corner, God can, and we should embrace his knowledge with grateful hearts."

She turned to him, studying the sharp features of his chiseled profile. "Thank you for helping me find my faith again. I'm learning our God isn't a small God. 'For my thoughts are not your thoughts, neither are your ways my ways, saith the Lord,'" she quoted.

Daniel accorded her a nod of approval as he guided the magnificent horses farther away from camp. They clattered across a wooden bridge, then turned on a forked road leading to the Colchester estate. "Isaiah 55:8. I've always loved that passage."

"Me too," she agreed with a smile.

She caught his look of pleasure, and held onto her smile.

He released the reins with one hand to briefly squeeze hers. "I am so pleased you agreed to meet Valentina and James. And all it took was a fortnight of refusals before you finally accepted a dinner invitation."

"One of the reasons I accepted this particular invitation was because I knew my time was running out."

"For what? To come up with more excuses?" he asked. "Why wouldn't you want to meet the Colchesters?"

"I'm ... I'm not a proper lady anymore." She glanced at him. "I'll forget how to act, what to say—"

"Be yourself. You're everything a lady should be—considerate and kind, and a woman with a sincere heart." He held up a hand when she shook her head. "And you're modest. But what I most love about you is that you're an original."

She shook her head. "I'm not worldly or sophisticated."

"A coquette feigning a blush never interested me."

Her heart hammered. So, he had now declared his interest in her, although of course she'd already assumed he was interested because of all the hours they spent together. She just hadn't known how much.

But he hadn't said he was in love with her ... or had he?

She lowered her lashes, but not before she caught the gleam in his eyes as his gaze roved over her. He was bent on using charismatic ways to enrapture her, and 'twas working.

Her cheeks were turning pink, and she didn't know where to look. She decided to inspect the toes of her boots.

'Twas easier to deal with him when they bantered, she decided, than when his expression heated with affection.

"What is your other reason?" he prompted.

"Other reason for what?"

"Refusing to meet the Colchesters despite my encouragement."

Her head jerked up. Her first impulse was to joke about his excellent memory in continuing their earlier conversation. In its place, she astonished herself by blurting out the truth. "You are leaving come the morrow, giving me no other choice."

"Your last chance to reenter English society?"

My last chance to be with you, she thought, although she merely nodded.

He guided the horses around the last bend, granting them a splendid view of remote hills and abundant, uncultivated moorlands. The carriage rocked comfortably beneath an arch of gnarled tree branches on the long driveway leading to the mansion.

As he pulled the horses to a smart stop at the entrance, he turned to her and beamed. "We're here."

Charity blinked rapidly. The grand house blazed with hundreds of flickering candles, and smoke billowed from the chimneys of numerous fireplaces. Pockmarks in the exterior stone walls boasted the resilience of enduring a harsh climate. In the distance, she heard the sound of waves hurtling against the rocky shoreline.

"Well, I'm hoping my news is good," Daniel was saying.

He was grinning, and she wondered what she'd missed as she'd gaped at the house. Her gaze narrowed with suspicion. "What news?"

"Penelope is leaving come the morrow. However, I decided to stay a while longer. Perhaps indefinitely."

"Why?"

"Why do you think, Charity?"

She contemplated him. His former amusement had been replaced with a look of such profound affection, it took her breath away.

Silence reigned for a beat as her brain processed the information.

He was staying because of her.

Feeling faint with happiness, she drew in a deep breath.

He reached out to tip up her chin, and his gaze locked with hers. "I lost you once and I can't lose you again." Slowly, he bent his head, and his lips parted hers for a long kiss. Without thinking, merely reacting, she twined her hands around his nape and welcomed his lips.

He responded to her yielding, kissing and cuddling her. When his lips finally left hers and their breathing slowed, he rested his forehead against hers. The heat of his body melted against her, and she felt love lighting the recesses of her heavy heart.

She touched her fingers to his beloved face and smiled into his eyes.

He smiled back. "Ready to reenter English society?"

Her stomach gave a funny little lurch. There was no mistaking the tenderness in his voice. And she'd repay him for his kindnesses by showing him she was truly the lady he believed her to be.

That is, if she could step out of the carriage without her legs collapsing beneath her, she thought, thinking about the formal evening ahead of her.

She again inhaled deeply, staring toward the house. "What if—"

"What if you dazzle them? Most assuredly, you will." He

went around the carriage, caught her by the waist and helped her down. A fine penetrating mist prompted her to wrap her shawl closer around her shoulders, a reminder that summer waned and fall quickly approached.

A footman bearing a torch emerged from the house, followed by a young servant, who bobbed a curtsy and introduced herself as Clare. A lisp slowed Clare's speech as she welcomed them.

Daniel inclined his head to thank Clare, then put his arm around Charity to give an encouraging squeeze. "My sister is anxious to see you, and James and Valentina are eager to meet you. I've spoken of you often."

So she'd been a subject of conversation. Could she live up to their expectations?

She turned a desperate look on him before she forced herself to think sensibly. Penelope was Daniel's sister. James Colchester was a London acquaintance. She could do this.

Nonetheless, would Valentina accept her as a Gypsy or Englishwoman? And what about James?

And Penelope? Charity had always felt Penelope disliked her. And from what she recollected, Penelope harbored a disdain for Gypsies, avoiding them by purposefully crossing the road if she spotted any. Perhaps she had changed. She had managed to stay at the Colchester home with Valentina for a fortnight.

Resolutely, Charity dismissed any negative thoughts while Daniel tucked her hand in the crook of his arm. Together, they walked up the mansion's stone steps, and their boots echoed on the slate floored hallway. She paused to admire the stucco entryway, the thick poplar beams, the portraits of Colchester ancestors hung on the walls. Truly, the home was one-of-a-kind.

She fought to keep her nerves under control, reminding herself that Valentina and James were Christians. If she faltered in conversation, surely she could talk about the Christian faith.

And Daniel had mentioned that James' son Jeremy was deaf. She was eager to meet and communicate with the little boy, although she assumed his nurse had probably already put him to bed.

Some other time, she hoped.

"Ready?" Daniel asked again.

"Aye." She squared her shoulders, hoping the cluster of nerves in her stomach would dissolve before she reached the parlor.

CHAPTER 7

*I*n the hour before dinner, Daniel sensed Charity's tenseness begin to ease as soon as she and Valentina exchanged appropriate greetings. With a wide smile, Valentina led her into the parlor, where she introduced Charity to her husband, James, and then settled into a linenfold chair beside her.

Penelope, already seated, offered only a faint inclination of her perfectly coiffed head. "So, the woman who caused her father so much grief has reappeared," she said. "Hello, Charity."

Visibly, Charity stiffened at Penelope's malicious remark, and turned to Daniel, her face pale, her expression strained.

"Don't be ridiculous," he snapped at Penelope, who met his cold stare with sham puzzlement.

"In my home," Valentina said, "judgements against others are not allowed." She threw a look of unwavering dislike toward Penelope. "We are all Christians and surely you know this Scripture from Matthew: 'Judge not, that ye be not judged.'"

To Daniel's disgust, his sister didn't apologize, nor even

bother to agree with Valentina. Instead, she merely glanced at a servant waiting in the doorway and indicated she wanted more sherry.

For Charity's sake, Daniel broke the uncomfortable silence by announcing that one of the dishes being served for dinner was cawl, a typical Welsh stew and ideal for a late-summer evening.

"And 'tis one of my husband's favorite dishes," Valentina said. "'Tis a stew made from meat and carrots and leeks. I've grown fond of it, just as James has grown fond of Romany roasted hedgehog." She glanced at her husband. "Aye?"

James chuckled imperturbably. His grey-eyed gaze lit with warmth as he looked at his wife. "Aye."

Spurred by Charity's agreement about the deliciousness of roasted hedgehog dredged in black pepper, Valentina bubbled on, recounting her childhood living in a Gypsy tribe with her sister, Yolanda, then her years as a drabardi, a fortune-teller, and how she became a Christian.

"Sometimes I believe God sent an angel to bless me. I thought I was powerless, but 'twas just the opposite. He gave me so much grace I became stronger, not weaker." Valentina cast another affectionate smile toward her husband, who stood with one shoulder propped against the fireplace. He raised his goblet to her, affectionately smiling at his radiant, ebony-haired wife.

Appearing a little bemused, Charity replied, "An angel is a wonderful idea, Valentina."

"We all have one, and your angel happens to be standing a foot away from you." Valentina peeked sidewise at Daniel. "In fact, I've noticed that your angel never takes his eyes off you." She leaned over to whisper in Charity's ear. "And he never stops talking about you, either."

Daniel grinned, overhearing Valentina's words.

His sister didn't appear nearly as enraptured by the

women's conversation. Instead, she leaned back in her chair and took swallow after swallow of the excellent sherry.

When dinner was announced, Daniel guided Charity into the dining room. The room was suffused with the delicious aroma of cawl stew.

Their host, James, sat at the head of the dining room table, with Valentina on his right and Penelope on his left. Charity sat next to Penelope, and Daniel took a seat across from Charity.

After they bowed their heads and said grace, the servant set bowls of the stew in front of everyone. As they began eating, Daniel gazed around the long dining room table, formally set with white damask linens, and then focused on the breathtakingly beautiful woman seated across from him. Glowing beeswax candles created a golden ambiance in the room, and Charity had never looked lovelier. Tonight, she was dressed in a soft, deep-purple gown. Her burnished ringlets were pulled back and framed her exquisite heart-shaped face.

As servants refilled wineglasses, and silver clinked against soup bowls, all five people seated at the table focused on the stew, except for him, because his gaze kept seeking Charity.

After six years, he thought, she was still slender, although her figure had blossomed. Her movements, always graceful, had become even more so, and her curves were enticing. Nature and the years had worked closely to produce a woman of extraordinary beauty. Thick black lashes edged her extraordinary eyes, reflecting crystal-blue when she was angry or indigo when she was sad.

Yet there was an elusive quality about her, as if she were a bird ready to take flight.

Charani, the Gypsy name that meant *bird,* was most appropriate. But even when she was younger, seemingly delighted with nature and everything life had to offer, she would land only long enough for a lively discussion with him. At the slightest risk of being captured, she'd become distant, her responses evasive. *And she'd fly away.*

All because of her father. Just thinking about the abuse she'd suffered at his hands made Daniel's fingers tighten around his wineglass. If only he'd known so he could have done something about it.

Nay, he silently chastised himself. He *should* have known something was wrong. He and Charity had been best friends. He had loved her then, a Christian-like love as well as the love of a friend, and he now felt incomparable sadness at the abuse she'd suffered.

He tried to concentrate on his meal, but again his gaze was drawn to her. Everything about her flowed like an unforgettable melody humming through his veins.

Because he loved her. They were soulmates. They were meant for each other.

His spoon stopped halfway to his mouth, as surprise and acknowledgement forced him to pause. This was more than a love for a friend. This was real.

James' voice caught his attention as he offered up a toast to Charity. Daniel raised his goblet, warmth radiating through his chest. Aye, he was totally and unequivocally in love with her.

She caught his gaze and smiled. He nodded reassurance and added a grin and a wink. They had been meant to meet again, here in Wales. God had brought them back together.

When the main course was cleared and the tablecloth taken away, sweetmeats, fresh fruit and ice cream were served.

Daniel leaned back in his chair and refused the sweet-meats. "No baked apples on the menu this evening?" he teased Valentina.

"Not tonight. You have told me often enough that baked

apples are your favorite dessert. Shall we plan on dining together tomorrow evening and I'll add them?" She gestured to Charity. "Will you join us? If you can come earlier in the day, you can meet Jeremy."

Charity vacillated, and Daniel was surprised. He assumed she would readily agree. Then again, his sister's icy silences, broken only by thinly-veiled insults at Charity, had cut through the meal's conversation. He assumed Charity had shrugged off the remarks, for she offered no rebuttals. From years past, she would have known Penelope's manner was difficult.

When dessert was finished, they rose and all complimented Valentina on an excellent meal. The men prepared to enjoy their glasses of port wine in the dining room, and the women to chat in the parlor. Afterwards, they'd come together again for tea and more conversation.

A perfect evening, Daniel mused. He'd be able to spend more time with Charity.

Penelope strolled to the dining room window, pushed back the heavy draperies and gazed at the nighttime sky. "Theodore will not be joining us after all," she informed the group. "He sent word he's no longer interested in the Welsh property, and we're returning to England immediately. If you'll excuse me, I'll take a walk by the garden and then retire. 'Twill be an early morning and I need a restful sleep." With that, she bid them a stiff good night.

Valentina, always the gracious hostess, met Penelope's moody stare with a smile. "I hope you enjoyed your stay here in Wales."

Silence reigned so thick that all movement in the room was momentarily suspended.

"Of course," Penelope finally replied.

"I'll walk in the gardens with you," Daniel said to his sister, as Valentina took Charity's hand and led her toward the parlor. "We won't be seeing each other for a while, as I'm intending to stay in Wales."

"You are welcome to stay here as long as you like," James said, and Valentina concurred.

Penelope didn't answer.

Daniel took her elbow in a firm grasp and steered her outdoors. He intended to upbraid her for the rude and unkind remarks she'd hurled at Charity. They were uncharitable and most uncalled for.

"Nay, Daniel." Penelope frowned at his hand on her elbow and drew back in the entryway. "I've changed my mind and have decided to head straight to bed."

"Nonsense. A stroll in the night air is ideal for a good night's rest." Tightening his hold, he pushed open the front door with his other hand, propelled her toward the garden, then abruptly dropped her arm.

"What was all that about in there with the Colchesters and Charity?" Fortified by his wrath, he raised his voice. "You were extraordinarily rude."

Outrage flew across Penelope's face. "You've become blind to reason, rhapsodizing about Wales ever since we arrived. And I blame that … that heathen woman. She's turned your feelings inside out and you're acting like a besotted fool."

"I already told you what Charity told me—she was forced to run away because of her father's cruelty."

"Mayhap." Penelope's fists clenched and then unclenched. "But by doing so, she caused him great harm. So much so that he lied about her whereabouts and said she was dead. What kind of Christian woman would do that, and then live like a vagrant all these years?"

CHAPTER 8

*P*enelope was wrong, of course.

Blind with anger, Daniel shouted that her tongue was venomous and he almost expected snakes to slither beneath them while she spoke. Then he stormed away, leaving her standing in the garden in speechless silence.

The hush of an ageless tomb settled on the carriage when he took Charity back to the Gypsy camp later that evening. Throughout the ride, he tried to convince her to go back to England with him and resume her previous life there. She stated, clearly and without reservation, that she'd never return.

"I'll see you come the morrow then," he said when he walked her to her tent. "We'll go riding."

Activity around the campfire was absent as he returned to the carriage and departed. In his frustration at his sister, at himself, and at Charity for not listening to reason, he failed to notice that the camp was almost empty and something was amiss.

At least, that was what he told himself when he returned late the following morning, filled with regret at the way he and Charity had parted the night before. When he rode his horse to the Gypsy campground, the tribe was gone. No tents, no wagons, the campfires cold.

In disbelief, he stared around at the empty place where the active tribe had stood with him the previous evening, when he'd come to take Charity to dinner. A group of people couldn't simply disband and leave everything in their lives that quickly. Could they?

He scratched his chin, reminding himself the Rom carried everything they needed with them. They hadn't left anything behind. Except him.

Where could they have gone? Surely not far, as they must've departed only hours earlier. He shaded his eyes and peered north, then east, south, then west. But in what direction were they traveling?

He swiftly rode back to the Colchesters' and strode into the house. The entry door slammed behind him. Alone in the parlor, he closed the door and considered the possibility that Charity had gone off with another man, that Gypsy. Daniel couldn't recall his name. Something about a pet. That contemplation was an unbearable and exasperating one. He couldn't believe she'd actually wed anyone but him.

As the minutes ticked by, he stood at the far end of the parlor and stared out the window at a rapidly fading afternoon.

"I thought you cared about me," he said into the empty room. His voice rose. "I thought you loved me! Why did you leave me again?" He shook his head. By insisting she move back to England, he had caused her to fly away again.

He strode to the sideboard and poured braggot into a goblet. He sipped, tasting a harsh defeat. What in the world was Charity doing, wandering all across Wales? Gypsies lived hand-to-mouth, and she'd once enjoyed a comfortable

English lifestyle. Wasn't she better off in England? Why, her behavior was infuriating and hardly made sense.

He took a long gulp of the braggot and then turned as the door behind him opened. He set the goblet on a side table as Valentina entered. She shut the door and then rushed to him, placing a hand on his arm.

"I know Luca's tribe departed this morning."

She didn't say how she knew, although as they'd talked one day at breakfast about Gypsy customs, she mentioned that the tribes relied on a *vurma,* a woman who knew the exact whereabouts of all the tribes. Now if only he knew where to find the *vurma.*

"Aye," he answered and looked away, unable to conjure up his usual ease with her.

Her hand tightened on his arm, forcing his gaze back to her. "I presume Charity went with them?"

Drawing a long breath, he curtly nodded.

"And you miss her?"

With a ragged sigh, he whispered, "Aye."

"Then I will come directly to the point. Why aren't you out looking for her?"

"I don't know where to look," he said quietly, trying not to flinch at the stabbing pain of loss in his heart. "This time she's disappeared for good. Last night when I took her back to the camp, I tried to force her hand and convince her to return to England." He trailed off, reached for his goblet and drained the braggot. "Why would God be so cruel ... to bring us together, only to rip us apart?"

"Mayhap what you believe God is doing to torment you is really using your circumstances to transform you. Sometimes God uses closed doors to lead you to the doors that are open."

He stared out the window as her words revealed the enormous mistake he'd made. Ever since he'd found Charity again, he'd assumed she wanted to resume her previous life in England. Despite the abuse she had revealed to him, he had believed she would welcome a return to the comfortable lifestyle she'd known—a fine house and plentiful food, parties and the opera, dancing in spacious, well-appointed drawing rooms. He hadn't stopped to consider that a simpler lifestyle suited her—as it suited him.

Valentina's voice drew his attention back to her. "Luca said he intended for the tribe to go south, where the warmer weather will last longer. He usually gravitates toward Swansea. 'Tis a market town, so he'll be able to barter any wares they've lifted from the townspeople here."

Daniel raised an eyebrow. "You must mean any wares they were *gifted* from the townspeople."

"Nay, I meant what I said. Lifted." Valentina met his gaze directly. "Soon, when you spend enough time with Charity, you will learn of the Rom's desperation. No one will give them work and so they must resort to stealing. You will realize they are not at fault." She subjected him to a long scrutiny. "Remember when we quoted the verse from Matthew last evening? There is another verse that has always been dear to my heart, because I stole many, many times, along with my fellow Rom when I lived with them."

"You stole?"

"Aye." Tears sprang to her eyes as she quoted, "'Judge not according to the appearance, but judge righteous judgement.'" She retied a bright-yellow handkerchief around her neck and walked to the parlor door. Opening it, she said, "Now go and find her."

* * *

THE RIDE TO SWANSEA, which Valentina had predicted would take three hours, took Daniel two and a half. Although the daylight hours of summer were long, a purple dusk was deepening as he reached the outskirts of the city.

He and Charity had been apart for less than twenty-four hours, and he missed her so much his chest ached.

'Twas more than her beauty that appealed to him. A captivating exuberance surrounded her, a mischievous approach to life despite her hardships. His mind understood the harsh reality of her absence, but his heart refused to accept a life without her. Even if she rejected him, he had to try.

When he found the Gypsy camp, they were still unloading heavy wagons and setting up tents. He tied his horse's reins to a tree, then wended his way around canvas and long poles and wooden trunks, searching for one head of red hair among the dark-haired Gypsies.

Luca greeted him with a quick nod and no friendliness. Other men regarded Daniel with stony expressions despite his courteous salutations. Kezia, however, rushed over to him and threw her arms around his waist.

"What took you so long?" she asked.

Although numerous replies formed on his lips, he stated the truth. "At first, I didn't know where to look."

Kezia's tiny fingers squeezed his arm as she guided him toward a tent located away from the others. "Charity has been so despondent this entire trip, I feared she'd never stop crying."

"She was crying?"

"Aye."

Feeling a pang of guilt so great he couldn't breathe, he lifted the opening to Charity's tent.

She sat on a wooden bench with her hands in her lap, her head bent. Wrapped in a gown of lavender wool, she looked like an angel, her shining copper-colored hair tumbling over her shoulders.

"Daniel?" Her crystal-blue eyes widened into huge orbs as she rose. Her generous lips parted into a slow smile.

He stepped forward. "Did I ever tell you that your smile lights up a room?'

"I don't know. Mayhap." She tilted up her chin. "Why are you here?"

"Because you're coming with me."

Her smile was replaced by a hurt, determined look. "Nay. I told you I'm not returning to England."

"Good, because neither am I."

Her hand was at her throat. "I—I don't understand. Exactly why are you here again?"

"I'm here because I love you." There. He felt better now that he'd said the words he should've spoken to her a fort-night ago.

He blew out a breath and waited. He also had to accept the fact that she may not love him.

She bit her lip in a combination of what looked like shyness and thoughtfulness, although he knew Charity would soon grow weary of cowering. She always confronted her reservations head-on.

He reached her and ran a forefinger over her delicate cheek. "I want us to make a life together."

She stepped back, shaking her head. "I can't return to my father, and you can't force me."

"Force you?" His hand stilled. Her face was so gorgeous, her expression so vulnerable, that he questioned himself for the thousandth time. How could he not have known of her mistreatment? Tenderly, he resumed caressing her cheek. "Your father is dead, Charity. He died soon after you ran away."

"Dead? My father …?" Briefly, she closed her eyes and drew in a shuddering breath. "You're not here to haul me back to England, to him? He did not send you to find me?"

His hands slid up and down her arms. "I'm here for only one reason. I love you. I've always loved you."

In the flickering glow of three lit candles on a wooden table, he saw expressions flit across her face—disbelief, sadness, and relief. "Daniel, I apologize for misjudging you." She tilted her head up, offering her mouth for his kiss. "I've always loved you too."

He kissed her, long and lingering, with all the desire and love he held in his heart. "Will you marry me?"

At his lips' urging she kissed him back, placing her slim fingers along his cheeks. "Aye," she whispered. "Aye."

"When? When will you marry me?"

She continued her exploration of his face and traced her fingers over his mouth. "A proper English wedding takes months to plan." She grinned at his frown. "Whereas a Romany Gypsy wedding takes only a day."

"I've waited six years." He fingered her curls, his pulse quickening at her nearness. "One more day is all I can manage. Who performs the ceremony?"

"Well, sometimes the leader of the tribe …" Her long fringe of black lashes flew up, and she regarded him with her clear blue eyes. "So, Luca—"

"As long as he doesn't cut my throat, then 'tis agreed. We can send for the Colchesters to attend the ceremony."

"Of course."

Appeased by the fact they'd wed come the morrow, he wrapped her in his arms. "And I hope you'll agree to live here in Wales. I've grown to love the country."

She slid her arms around his neck, molded herself to his length, and lightly kissed him. "As do I."

"Good. I've made a decision to purchase a country estate. 'Tis a three hour ride from Swansea, and the property needs a bit of work."

Aye, a neutral phrase for a grand undertaking, he thought.

She grinned. "Sounds perfect."

He gazed at his beautiful bride-to-be and thanked God. He had separated them for a while, but He'd also given them abundant grace and made them stronger. They had realized a deeper love, as well as an appreciation for each other that they would never have known otherwise.

"Daniel?" Charity was asking. "So you're agreeable to a Romany wedding ceremony?"

"Of course," he murmured. He kissed her again. He couldn't get enough of her.

"Do you even know what a Gypsy ceremony involves?"

"Nay." Distracted by her stunning smile, he grazed his lips over hers, savoring the exquisite taste of her.

"You'll learn of the ceremony come the morrow then," she said. "Do you have a broomstick handy?"

THE END

A NOTE FROM JOSIE

Dear Friend,

Thank you for reading *Seeking Charity.* I hope you enjoyed it. *Seeking Charity* is the second book in my Inspirational Regency romance "Seeking" series.

The Romany Gypsy culture is complex and fascinating. After researching their traditions and beliefs, I wanted to write stories focusing on bigotry during the Regency era.

Charity Weston, with her copper-colored hair and crystal-blue eyes, is a complex heroine. Running away at a young age, she joins a Romany Gypsy tribe.

Daniel Hayward, the hero, is a wealthy Englishman, and a devout Christian with a kind heart.

My hope is that this story will make you believe again in second-chance love and God's grace.

The Romany Regency Inspirational romances begins with Valentina and James in *Seeking Fortune*, and Seeking Charity is the second book. The series continues with Luca and Patience in *Seeking Patience.*

Seeking Rachel, is the fourth book in the series.

Although not part of the Regency Inspirational series, my

Tudor short story, *Seeking Catherine*, featuring a Romany Gypsy hero, is always free.

If you loved this inspirational romance as much as I loved writing it, please help other people find *Seeking Charity* by posting your amazing review, as well as for the bundle: The Seeking Series

Seeking Charity is available in ebook, paperback, Large Print paperback, Hardcover, and audiobook.

I'd love to meet you in person someday, but in the meantime, all I can offer is a sincere and grateful thank you. Without your support, my books would not be possible.

As I write my next sweet or inspirational romance, remember this: Have you ever tried something you were afraid to try because it mattered so much to you? I did, when I started writing. Take the chance, and just do something you love.

My Spotify Play List for Seeking Charity is here.

With sincere appreciation,

Josie Riviera

Want more Inspirational romances?

Regency:
Seeking Fortune
Seeking Patience
Seeking Rachel
The Seeking Series

Contemporary:
Cherish Hearts 6 Book Bundle
Holly's Gift

RECIPE FOR TRADITIONAL
WELSH CAWL STEW

Ingredients:

Approximately 2 ½ lbs. lamb, beef or ham
1 chopped onion
6 peeled and chopped potatoes
3 peeled and chopped carrots
2 peeled and chopped parsnips
2 washed and peeled leeks
fresh parsley
vegetable stock
salt and pepper
Place meat in large pot, cover with water and bring to

boil. Let simmer for 3 hours. Leave in refrigerator overnight to cool. The following day, skim off any fat.

Cut the meat and return to stock. Add potatoes, carrots and parsnips. Simmer until done and season with salt and pepper. Add leeks and parsley just before serving.

Enjoy for lunch or dinner with crusty bread.

SEEKING PATIENCE CHAPTER ONE PREVIEW

hapter One
England, 1813

LUCA BOLDOR HAD MADE A MISTAKE—A *big* mistake.

"May God strike you all," he swore under his breath at the murderous band of rival Roma tribesmen gaining on him, ready to attack. He'd merely been looking for food for his tribe.

He pulled his ragged overcoat around his shoulders and made his getaway through the snow. Snowflakes fell thick and heavy, twice as fast as earlier that evening. Wind carried the drifts in wayward, wispy circles and thankfully concealed his tracks.

He could escape unseen. He'd become good at that.

Slipping on a patch of ice, he stumbled and hit the ground face first.

His voice broke in agony. He stifled a scream, because a man never screamed. Certainly not a Roma man.

Relying on sheer muscle to raise the lower half of his body, he dug his elbows into the gritty, wet snow and crawled forward. Aye, a man didn't crawl, either.

But sometimes a man made exceptions to his own rules.

Advancing shadows split the stretches of dull white snow. Desperately, he searched his surroundings, knowing he was too easy to find. His body ached with the pain of a cruel beating. His breath, so cold a moment ago, burned in his chest.

Give up. But the thought was so inconceivable that Luca pushed it from his mind.

Instead, he envisioned the elders of his tribe foraging for food. They'd starve without his hunting skills and perish in a sennight. If he could only get them through another winter, he could improve their lot by moving them to the coast. Food was more plentiful by the sea and they wouldn't need to steal to survive.

Heavy footsteps crunched through the snow and Luca risked a swift glance over his shoulder. Marko, the leader of the rival tribe, and his men drew closer.

Blind panic rushed through Luca's limbs.

Past a swell of blackthorn trees, he spotted a ravine. He dropped to his knees and burrowed into the snow. Faster. Deeper. His nerves pinched in short, silent spasms.

Curse the frost for numbing his fingers. Curse his senses for deserting him. Curse the whole, damn, uncaring world.

He lowered himself into the hole and threw brittle tree branches on top. Then he peered through the branches and waited. The bleary figures of Marko and his tribesmen approached. A glimmer of moonlight lit the darkness and threatened to expose Luca's meager covering.

A persistent voice whispered in his mind. *Run. There's time. They won't see you.*

He grimaced. His restless body shifted. His battered leg stiffened, a reminder of his helplessness.

"Luca won't escape me." Marko's rough tone severed the cold night air. "He claims he disappears like a spirit, but he's just a man."

A few men snickered uneasily and Luca recognized their voices. Killing was a sport for them. Despite the numbness, tiny hairs on Luca's nape stood on end.

Marko's booted toes stopped within a few feet of Luca's makeshift hole. The stench of his unwashed body filled Luca's nostrils and he held his breath until he thought his lungs would burst. His eyes watered from the cold, but he kept his gaze on Marko.

"Nadya is my woman and they've been meeting secretly for months. She was hiding our food and giving it to him."

Marko didn't speak, he growled. Despite the cold, he wiped his sweaty face with dirty gloves, then kicked the blackthorn trees, rustling the brittle branches of Luca's covering. "No one betrays me. Nadya learned her lesson quick, and he will, too."

In silent rage, Luca squeezed his eyes shut to blot the unsettling images racing through his mind. If he'd known that Marko was going to beat Nadya, Luca would've stayed and tried to protect her. When Marko and his men had stormed into Nadya's tent, Luca had fought them, then gotten away. He knew his strength would be no match for a tribe of enraged, jealous Roma.

Luca tightened his fists, defying the impulse to shake off the burdensome branches and pummel the rival lord's head into the snow. He'd not allow Marko to escape punishment for senselessly abusing a woman.

Nay. Not now. He swallowed to quell the pain feeding his anger.

He was a half-breed—half-English, half-Romany. And when his strength returned, he'd seek justice the Romany way—swift and sure.

At thirty years old, he was a leader. A legend to fear.

"Nanosh," Marko shouted to one of his men, "We'll resume our search at sunrise. It's too dark to continue." Marko's footsteps receded. His men obeyed without complaint.

Luca waited an interminable minute before he pushed the branches off his snowy covering. He heaved his body out of the hole and sucked in a sharp groan at the needle-like pain piercing his leg. Then he crawled away from Marko and his men like a helpless, despicable cripple.

If he didn't find shelter soon, he might lose his leg. Then he'd no longer command the respect of his tribe. Then he'd sink deeper in his English father's eyes—if such a thing were possible. Then...Hell, then he might as well die, because there'd be nothing left if he were a broken and helpless cripple.

Every few feet, Luca stopped to catch his ragged breath and control the shivers wracking his limbs. He tried to flex his fingers but they had no feeling, stiff and frozen sticks that hardly moved. Wryly, he thought about the leather hawking gloves, an unexpected treasure he'd found on a dirt road months before. The English dandy who'd dropped the gloves in a busy London marketplace never missed a step, never bent to search for them. Just kept walking, probably to Bond Street where he could spend more coin, while his rich, ruby cloak billowed behind him.

Those precious, warm gloves. All smooth black leather and cream silk lining.

Luca had left the gloves back at his camp for an elderly tribesman to wear.

Wryly, Luca shook his head. He'd assured the tribesman he wouldn't need the gloves, but foresight had never been his forte. Throughout the night, he'd pondered the ironic joke the fates had played on him as he blew on his cold hands.

He crawled, then limped through the snow, grabbing a tree branch to steady his gait. Beyond, a large, ungated home loomed. He focused on the flicker of oil lamps in the windows, the tall chimneys standing as sentinels on either side of the house.

He'd reached the outskirts of Ipswich.

He gripped the tree branch tighter, the icy bark biting into his fingers.

He should never have led his tribe here. This town always brought bad luck, much as it had brought bad luck to his Romany mother.

A weighty sigh brought an unanticipated heaviness to his chest. His mother would've loved being a proper hostess in a fine house such as this, serving tea with hot, buttered buns to her guests while she sat on a cushioned settee. Why hadn't he been able to give her these things?

The wintry wind swirled his cloak around him. He slumped against the tree, his torn boots sinking into the snow, soaking his feet. He wiped the wet snowflakes from his cheeks.

He still remembered his mother's fragrance, bergamot and roses, the precious oils she dabbed on her wrists each morning. Her soft voice still resonated in his chest, whispering of love, and beauty, and happier days. And then she'd died, abandoning him, and he'd struggled and sparred his way to adulthood.

"A plague on the English," he whispered, knowing the haughty aristocrats living in the grand home couldn't hear him. He loathed the idly rich and the privileged life they led, the desperation giving him no choice but to seek their favor.

"Luca."

His legs gave out. Dropping the tree branch, Luca fell to his knees and peered upward. The voice above him sounded youthful, deep, and familiar. He clawed through his hazy thoughts, trying to remember the child's name.

"I followed you out of Marko's camp. I know you were trying to get food for our tribe."

Luca kept his attention on the boy, his dearest friend since the boy was a child. "Pulko?"

He heard his own voice, slurring, sounding weak.

Tears streamed down the boy's face, despite a hasty swipe at his cheeks.

"Stop crying." Luca didn't have the strength to give the boy his usual friendly cuff because he needed to lift his arms, and his arms prevented his upper body from collapsing.

Pulko mopped the scraggly whiskers on his chin with his

ragged blue cloak. "No one saw me. I'm fast and stayed hidden in the trees."

"Circle back to the tribe. Your mother will worry if you're missing."

"She's asleep." Pulko crouched beside Luca. "I'll stay with you."

Luca's palms flattened into the snow. "Your foolishness endangers the entire tribe. You'll give away my position."

"I won't abandon you," Pulko said. "I'll protect you."

"Protect the tribe. I don't need anyone."

Pulko hunched into his overcoat, his long dark hair flapping in the blustery weather. He paced, making a line of large footprints in the snow. "Marko will kill you if he finds you."

* * *

*** End of excerpt *Seeking Patience* by Josie Riviera
Copyright © 2016 Josie Riviera
***

READ the rest of Luca and Patience's Story
   Pick up your copy of *Seeking Patience* today!
   FREE on Kindle Unlimited!

ALSO GRAB:
   The Seeking Series

Savor the magic of the Romany Gypsies with this collection of three Regency Christian romances in my exclusive set.

Find out why readers are falling in love with The Seeking Series & staying up all night reading! These sweet, inspirational romances will warm your heart.

Free on Kindle Unlimited.

ABOUT THE AUTHOR

USA TODAY bestselling author, Josie Riviera, writes Historical, Inspirational, and Sweet Romances. She lives in the Charlotte, NC, area with her wonderfully supportive husband. They share their home with an adorable shih tzu, who constantly needs grooming, and live in an old house forever needing renovations.

To receive my Newsletter and your free sweet romance novella ebook as a thank you gift, sign up <u>HERE.</u>

Join my Read and Review VIP Facebook group for exclusive giveaways and ARCs.

To connect with Josie, visit her website and sign up for her newsletter. As a thank-you, she'll send you a free sweet romance novella.

josieriviera.com/
josieriviera@aol.com

ACKNOWLEDGMENTS

An appreciative thank you to my patient husband, Dave, and our three wonderful children.

ALSO BY JOSIE RIVIERA

Valentine Hearts Boxed Set

1-800-CUPID

1-800-CHRISTMAS

1-800-IRELAND

1-800-SUMMER

1-800-NEW YEAR

The 1-800-Series Sweet Contemporary Romance Bundle

Irish Hearts Sweet Romance Bundle

Holly's Gift

A Chocolate-Box Valentine

A Chocolate-Box Christmas

A Chocolate-Box New Years

A Chocolate-Box Summer Breeze

A Chocolate-Box Christmas Wish

A Chocolate-Box Irish Wedding

Chocolate-Box Hearts

Chocolate-Box Hearts Volume Two

Chocolate-Box Double Hearts

Recipes from the Heart

Leading Hearts

New Year Hearts

SENIOR HEARTS

A Summer To Cherish

Summer Hearts

Romance Stories To Cherish Volume Two

Cherished Hearts

Christmas in the Air

A Very Christian Christmas

The 1-800-Series Volume Two

Christmas Tails of the Heart

Cocoa's Christmas Love

Pawfect Christmas Hearts

Pink Coral Island

Most books are available in ebook, audiobook, paperback, Large Print paperback and Hardcover.

Many are FREE on Kindle Unlimited!